Too Good to be True

MARG MCALISTER

BLUE GEM PUBLISHING

This edition published by Blue Gem Publishing in 2022.

Text and copyright © Marg McAlister 2015

Title: Too Good to be True | Marg McAlister, author

ISBN: 978-1-922772-33-6 (Paperback edition)

ISBN: 978-0-9945205-5-5 (Ebook edition)

Cover Design by Annie Moril

V27032022

ALSO BY MARG McALISTER

The Ugly Duckling

Perched on a camp chair near Georgie's gypsy trailer was a stocky girl of about thirteen, with short-cropped medium brown hair tied up with a fifties bandana. She was clad in a fitted striped shirt in navy and white and high-waist dark blue cropped pants, with matching ballet flats that she had kicked off so she could draw her knees up under her chin. Her eyes were fixed on the photoshoot in action near a gleaming ruby-red 1957 Chevy Belair automobile and its cheerful matching Shasta trailer.

No wonder she was entranced, Georgie thought, following her gaze. The scene she was watching was like an ad for the perfect fifties family, emphasizing 'perfect'. The woman was Madelyn Draper, and she had nailed the iconic Grace Kelly look: blonde hair swept back from her forehead and falling in casual waves to her shoulders; fitted short-sleeved sweater with the matching cardigan draped over her shoulders; a full skirt swirling around toned legs. As Georgie watched, Madelyn removed her cat-eye sunglasses. She treated the cameras to a charming smile, putting her arm around her enchanting golden-haired daughter Elizabeth and drawing her close. Elizabeth looked good enough to eat in a candy pink swing skirt, a high ponytail, and a lollipop-striped top.

Standing next to Madelyn was the most perfect male Georgie had ever set eyes on. She knew who he was: everyone in vintage circles did. Jonathan Draper, age twenty-five, mega-eligible bachelor and renowned playboy. He reminded her a little of her brother Jerry, except he was even more good-looking. He angled his chiseled jaw toward the camera, obeyed the photographers' yelled requests to rest a hand on his mother's shoulder, and flashed a wink in his sister's direction.

On the other side of young Elizabeth stood Madelyn's husband, Douglas Draper, CEO of Draper Games. He looked nothing like his wife or children. Douglas had a homely, lived-in face that was creased in lines of permanent good humor. Known for being a good sport who would go along with his wife's whims as long as he could indulge his twin passions of vintage automobiles and computer games, he had donned conservative fifties gear and was obediently following instructions to pose, smile, and interact with his family.

There were two members of the family missing. One was the eldest son, Richard, around a year older than Jonathan and estranged from the family. Georgie had heard rumors that ranged from drug use to petty theft, but nobody was quite sure.

The other person not in the photoshoot was Elizabeth's fraternal twin, Charlotte, and she was the one sitting outside Georgie's trailer.

When Georgie looked back at Charlotte, the girl's eyes were focused directly on her, watching her approach.

Georgie sat in the camp chair next to the girl and grinned. "Opting out of the family photos, Charlotte?"

"Charlie, if you don't mind," the girl said politely, not seeming at all surprised that Georgie knew who she was. "And I don't think they'll miss me."

Georgie nodded, studying the girl while appearing not to. "Well, some people are into publicity; some aren't." Just as she had heard rumors about the missing brother Richard, she had picked up the odd snippet of information about Charlotte. The ugly duckling, people said—the girl her mother tended to hide away. Georgie had heard she was moody and uncommunicative. Almost antisocial.

Ugly duckling might be a bit harsh, but the girl was plain, no doubt about it. She looked like a pocket-sized version of her father. Homely, with clear dark gray eyes that looked as though they could see right through artifice of any kind.

Including Georgie. The girl knew perfectly well that she was under scrutiny. "I think I might be a bit like you," she said. "Your father and brother are always on TV in the Johnny B. Goode RV Empire ads, but you aren't. Except for the time you were all on the news when that weirdo who was stalking Jaxx Saxby set fire to your trailer."

Georgie gave a wry smile and glanced at her new home on wheels. Her father had offered to make it bigger, better, with more storage and tricky little compartments and heaven knows what else, but she had said no. She wanted one just like the old one.

Which was precisely what she got. Apart from the paint being a bit shinier, you wouldn't know the difference. And thanks to her friends Tammy and Layla, who had moved heaven and earth to find the same bedspread and fabrics, she had felt instantly at home.

"I like your trailer," Charlie said, following her gaze. "I saw some pictures of the old one, and this looks just the same."

"As close as we could get it." Georgie nodded over toward the Draper family's vintage trailer, where Madelyn was now opening the door and beckoning the cameramen to look inside. "That's a beautiful Shasta you've got there, too. Not one of ours, though—your dad likes to restore vintage cars and trailers himself, doesn't he?"

"Yes. He says he's a purist. Every little detail has to be right." There was affection in Charlie's voice as she spoke. "He does a lot of the work on them himself, you know. People think he just pays others to do it, but he likes it. He lets me help him, sometimes."

Georgie could imagine Charlie getting to work stripping back old surfaces and cutting out rot. Her mother and sister, maybe not so much. "What about Elizabeth? Does she help too?"

"No. Beth doesn't like getting dirty. She likes it when they're all finished, and she can dress up for the vintage rallies." Charlie laughed, watching her sister hamming it up for the cameras. "Like now."

When she laughed, her whole face lit up. Definitely not an ugly duckling, Georgie thought. The girl had a face full of character, like her father. She would end up with the same laughter lines. She was certainly not taciturn or antisocial, either, judging by the current conversation.

"I'm taking some time out, making a cup of tea," Georgie said, taking the initiative. "Can I offer you something to drink?"

Charlie slid her feet off the seat and into her ballet flats, not waiting to be asked twice. "Thanks. I'd *love* to see the inside of your trailer. I've seen pictures of it in the vintage trailer magazine, but it's always better to see the real thing."

"Come on then. I love showing it off." Georgie stood up and led the way, curious. So far, Charlie hadn't given any sign of having a reason for being there, but Georgie had a feeling that there was one. It wasn't just a coincidence that the girl had picked one of the camp chairs outside her distinctive gypsy trailer.

Charlie's face became even more animated when she stepped inside. "Oh! I love it. I knew I would." She wandered around, running her fingers over the carved rails of the shelves and casting admiring glances at the stained glass inserts, while Georgie put the kettle on and fetched a soda for her guest.

Charlie paused when she saw the crystal ball, covered in its black velvet cloth. She reached out and touched the fabric with hesitant fingertips. "I know what this is. I read that your great-grandma asked your father to rescue it. Did she *know?*"

"She didn't foresee everything that was going to happen," Georgie said. "Otherwise, we would have prevented it. She just had a strong urge to see the crystal ball. She doesn't ignore feelings like that."

Charlie nodded and continued her inspection of the trailer. When she reached the bed, she smoothed her fingers over the rich embroidered bedspread. "This is beautiful. Is it just the same as the old one?"

"Just the same."

The girl looked down to the carved pedestal base for the bed. "I remember reading that you had sort of hidden storage under the bed."

Georgie was amused. "That's right. It's okay to look. See that carving on the right? The bird's head? Push it in."

Intrigued, Charlie did so and laughed with delight when a deep drawer with several compartments glided silently open. "This is so cool!" She closed it, and then opened it again. "Did you design this?"

"My father did. He's clever that way."

"So's my dad. That's why I like working with him, but he never puts in anything that wasn't in the original. That's why my mother doesn't like staying in real vintage trailers. She says she likes mod cons. She wants to buy one of the modern fakes from the RV Empire, but Dad won't let her."

Georgie hid a smile at the term 'modern fakes' and showed Charlie a few more of the unique touches her father had added. It was a pleasure to share it with someone so genuinely interested.

"You really like all this, don't you?" she said finally, waving to the table. "Sit down, Charlie, while I make the tea." She poured hot water into the teapot and took it to the table.

"I want to do it for a living," Charlie said, sipping her soda. "Restore cars and trailers. I told my dad."

"Is that why you're here to see me? To find out more about it?"

There was a brief silence, then Charlie said, "No, not exactly."

"Oh?" Georgie slid into the seat opposite. "What, then?"

Charlie turned the glass around and around, staring at the bubbles before she raised her eyes to Georgie's.

"I want you to find out the truth about my

brother." She jerked her head towards the door in the general direction of her family outside. "Not *him.* Not Jonathan. My other brother. I need to prove that Ricky didn't do what they said he did."

CHAPTER 2

A Tale of Woe

Charlie's eyes held Georgie's as she spoke, and her chin lifted just a little. There was a defiant spark in her eyes and tension in her stance. She might as well have said out loud; I'm *ready to fight on this one.*

"I see," Georgie said, not looking away. "And why do you think I can help, Charlie?"

"I've read about you. I've Googled you." Charlie's gray eyes practically drilled through Georgie. "Some people say you're a fraud, but when I looked at their Facebook pages and checked them out, they're mostly the kind of people who would say any fortune teller or psychic was a fraud. I read every article I could find about you. I looked at your Facebook friends. I think you're the real deal."

"Oh," Georgie said faintly, somewhat bemused.

"OK. That's good. But what do you think I can do?"

Charlie's penetrating gaze finally moved away from Georgie to the crystal ball, hidden in the shadows on the shelf. "Just what I said. Please help me get to the truth. Look into your crystal ball and tell me what you see."

She's still tense, Georgie thought. Whatever had happened to Charlie's brother Ricky – Richard? – it was tearing this child apart.

"I know what you're thinking," Charlie said. "That I'm just a kid. I don't know what I'm talking about. But I *do*. I know my brother, and he wouldn't do this. You've *got* to help me." On the last few words, her voice cracked, and there was a momentary sheen of tears in her eyes. Then she looked away, and Georgie could see her shutting down the emotion, retaking control.

This was a strong little girl. Hurting, but strong.

"Charlie…" Georgie reached out and touched her hand. "I want to help. Really, I do. But let me be honest with you, I don't know how we stand with the law, my helping a girl of…how old are you?"

"Almost thirteen. It's our birthday in two weeks, and I want Ricky to be there."

Our birthday. Of course, she and the lovely Elizabeth were twins.

"You mean he won't come to your birthday?" Then Georgie amended it to: "Or *can't*, maybe?"

"My mother won't let him in the house. My father might, but he's no match for my mother once she makes up her mind. But he didn't *do* it!"

Georgie put both elbows on the table and massaged her forehead. A child was begging for help. She couldn't say no.

She thought of Grace, another child that had come to see her and who had helped turn things around. Wisdom could come at any age.

"All right. Here's the deal, Charlie. I'll see what I can find out, but let's keep it between ourselves that you're here to see me in my capacity as a fortune-teller, OK?" She gestured around at the trailer. "If anyone asks, you're here asking me about the construction of my gypsy caravan."

"Sure." Momentarily diverted, she asked: "Why do you call it a caravan?"

"Because of its European heritage. They call it a caravan, so I sometimes do too. It's just a thing I have about it."

"Then I will too, from now on," Charlie said.

"Thank you." Georgie smiled at her. "See if you can convince others to do the same."

Charlie nodded and then sat up a little

straighter, a light of determination in her eyes. "Can we talk about Ricky now?"

Georgie stood up and walked the two steps across the trailer to lift the crystal ball down from its shelf. She couldn't help rubbing her hands lovingly over the globe beneath the black velvet as she carried it to the table; she had come so close to losing it in the fire. Thank God her great grandmother Rosa had followed her instincts to make sure it was safe.

Charlie watched, mesmerized, as Georgie uncovered the crystal ball and set it down between them. "What now?"

"Think about your brother. Focus on whatever is worrying you, and let's see what comes up." She glanced at the girl's tense face. "Relax, Charlie. Cast aside any feelings of anger and fear, and just think of Richard."

"Ricky. It's only my mother and Jon that call him Richard."

"Ricky. Just breathe slowly and evenly, and think of Ricky."

The crystal ball was not perfect—in fact, it was a long way from it. In the early days, when she was still feeling her way, Georgie often became frustrated when it refused to give up its secrets. Now she took it more philosophically. When the time was right, what was necessary would be revealed.

This time, however, it was cooperating. Georgie felt the familiar inner sense of excitement that presaged some sort of revelation. It was accompanied by that odd feeling of warmth that also went along with a glimpse into the future—or the past.

She wasn't going to have to disappoint Charlie, but she just hoped that the information that came through was what the girl so desperately wanted. What if Ricky was guilty of everything they'd said?

Opposite her, Charlie shifted in her seat, her eyes glued to the crystal ball. "It's going all smoky," she whispered, as though afraid that it would all go away if she spoke out loud. "Is that good?"

"Yes, it's good. It means that something is coming through."

Charlie sucked in a low, slow breath and closed her eyes. Georgie could *feel* her concentration.

The wisps of white mist in the crystal ball writhed in a slow dance, but nothing more was revealed. No images. Nothing. Georgie could see that Charlie's tense fingers, locked together, were as white as the mist.

Then, slowly, there was a tiny *blip* in Georgie's mind, and she had the sense of a door opening. Still no images—she had no idea what Ricky looked like

—but a trickle of understanding that rapidly became a fast-flowing stream of impressions.

She never knew how this would work. She would get images at one reading; she'd see words or hear spoken words the next. And then sometimes, like today, she would just *know*—*ideas*, sensations, understanding.

The life of a fortune-teller wasn't anything like what most people thought.

Finally, acutely aware of Charlie's angst, she spoke.

"Your brother. Ricky. He's living alone, in a small space somewhere. An apartment...no, not an apartment. But it's small. Not a trailer, and not a boat, because I don't sense water. It's...different."

"He lives in a converted train carriage. On a property backing on to an old railway siding." Charlie's eyes flew open, and her voice held excitement and hope.

"Yes, that works. He's..." for a moment, Georgie debated on how much to share with the girl but made an instant decision to treat her with the respect she deserved. "He's despondent, and there's a lot of simmering anger. He has made a few missteps in life, and he doesn't know how to fix it."

"He has, I guess." Charlie's voice held resentment. "But nothing *like* what they said he did. I *know* Ricky."

"You're right. I can sense that." Georgie sifted through the swirling impressions that were flowing in. "He misses you and misses his father. He is at odds with his brother and his mother."

"He's always fought with Jonathan, and my mother's always on Jon's side. Because Jon's the younger brother, you see."

Georgie did see. She'd suffered at the hands of her older brother Jerry all her life—smooth-talking, fast-thinking, handsome Jerry, who had managed to twist anything to make himself sound like the injured party or the smart one. She pictured the even more handsome and probably clever Jonathan Draper and imagined him doctoring the facts to suit himself.

"So when Ricky took these…missteps… your mother wasn't surprised?"

"Sort of." Charlie hesitated. "Do you want to know what happened?"

"In a minute." Georgie held up a hand, still somewhat at a distance, trying to make sense of what was coming in. Something about gems… jewelry…She exhaled. slowly. "Do I see some sort of trouble with the law? Was Ricky charged? Or incarcerated?"

"No. Yes. I mean, yes, he was accused of stealing, and the police interviewed him, but Dad and Mom covered it up. Not that it helped much because everyone seems to know about it."

"I see." Georgie was silent for a moment, looking within and trying to identify the underlying message.

Injustice, she thought.

She didn't know Ricky, and she had met his sister only fifteen minutes before, but there were grounds for Charlie's belief that he was innocent. She had learned to trust her instincts, and they were telling her that there was a lot more to the Ricky situation than it appeared.

"Is that all?" Charlie was looking at her hopefully. "Can you see what really happened?"

Georgie looked across at her, the plain little face with honest gray eyes and goodness radiating from her. A lovely little girl.

"Tell me more about the missing jewelry, Charlie. Did they find it in Ricky's possession?"

"No, it was in a pawn shop. One that he had used before, in the next county, when he was a teenager."

Georgie was puzzled. The Draper family was loaded—why would the teenage Ricky need to pawn his belongings? Unless he wanted money for something that his father wouldn't cough up for.

Like drugs. The answer popped into her head, so she went with it.

"Was Ricky ever involved with drugs, Charlie? As far as you know?"

"You saw it, didn't you?" Charlie nodded at the crystal ball. "In there. It was only for a while when he was a teenager and mostly weed. That's what Ricky says, and I believe him."

"That's why he pawned his stuff?"

"Just some computer games. Dad was furious. He got them back." She gnawed at a fingernail, and Georgie noticed that they were all bitten down to the quick. "I know this sounds bad. He pawned his stuff because Mom cut off his allowance after he sneaked out a few times. Now Mom says she can't trust him anymore, but I do."

"I can see that. That's why you're here." Georgie smiled at her, wanting to take away the bleak look in the girl's eyes. "For what it's worth, Charlie, I have a strong feeling that Ricky is innocent—but to find out more, I probably need to see him. Do you think he'd be up for that?"

"If I ask him, he will. But don't—"

Her words were interrupted by a male voice calling from outside. "Charlotte! Are you in there?"

Charlie's eyes narrowed, and in one swift movement, she picked up the black velvet cloth and flicked it over the crystal ball, hiding it. "Don't tell him I was asking you about Ricky," she begged in an undertone and then bounded to her feet and went to the door.

"Jon! Yes, I'm in here. You should *see* this trailer; it's amazing! But Georgie says we should call it a caravan." She looked back, her eyes pleading. "Can Jon and Beth come and have a look too, Georgie?"

"Of course." By all means, thought Georgie. She was keen to meet the other members of the Draper family. Who knew what she might pick up?

CHAPTER 3

The Drapers

Jonathan Draper led the way, with Charlie's twin, Elizabeth, laughingly pushing at his back to hurry him up. "Come on, Jonathan! I want to see!"

He ducked his head to come inside and beamed at Georgie, offering a hand, radiating friendliness and charm. "Hello."

For a moment, Georgie blinked: he was just too good to be true. *Nobody* could be this good-looking. Up close, Jonathan was a force to be reckoned with. His thick blonde hair was brushed back in a wavy pompadour to suit his casual fifties outfit, which looked better on him than on anyone Georgie had ever seen, including her annoyingly handsome brother Jerry. His eyes, the color of light sherry, shone with good humor, and his wide grin pushed twin dimples into his cheeks. "I hope you'll forgive the intrusion. No doubt Charlotte has been bugging you about every detail." He looked around him admiringly. "Nice trailer!"

She couldn't help but smile back, shaking his hand. His grip was firm but not a bone-breaker.

Elizabeth squeezed around him, her cheerful little blonde ponytail bouncing in excitement. "Let me in, Jonathan." She gave her twin a friendly poke on the arm. "I saw you sneaking in here, Charlie, but they wouldn't let me come across until the photos were done."

Georgie looked from Jonathan to Elizabeth. They were clearly brother and sister: the same regular features and the same tawny eyes; the same blonde hair—both impossibly good-looking.

Next to her siblings, Charlie looked plainer than ever. Georgie felt a pang of sympathy. No doubt the child had overheard unfavorable comparisons; that was how it usually went when a pretty child had a plain-Jane sister.

"There's some beautiful work here." Jonathan was bending over to examine the carved railing. "Hand-carved?"

"Yes." Georgie was impressed that he even noticed. Charlie had exclaimed over it, too, but she knew a lot about restoration and quality work from working with her father.

"Look at this, Jon." Charlie moved across to the bed, her hand hovering over the bird's carved head that opened the drawer in the pedestal, and glanced at Georgie for permission. "Can I show them, Georgie?"

"Be my guest." Enjoying the child's delight, which reflected Georgie's feelings the first time she had seen the Vardo, she watched while Charlie demonstrated the hidden drawer.

Elizabeth tugged at her twin. "Can I have a turn?"

The two girls exchanged identical grins, and Charlie moved aside to let her sister try it. "Just push it gently, Bethie."

They have the same smile, thought Georgie. It was the only point of similarity, and it was Charlie's best feature. When she smiled with genuine warmth, her face became interesting.

Perhaps she would grow into her looks.

She saw that Jonathan was watching them too, but then he glanced across at Georgie as though sensing her eyes on him. "Elizabeth doesn't share Charlotte's interest in renovating old trailers," he said, with a slight smile. "She likes to play in them when they're done, though."

"That's what I told her," Charlie said.

For the next few minutes, Charlie pointed out Georgie's home's various features to Jonathan and Elizabeth until her brother angled his wrist to look at his watch. "Sorry, girls, we have to go. Mom wants you over there to help serve morning tea at her new trailer."

"Not more photos," Charlie said immediately, her brows drawing together in a frown. The action made her look like a cranky troll.

"Don't do that, Charlotte." Jonathan flicked her on the nose, smiling to take away the sting. "If the wind changes, you'll get stuck."

"Stop it." She slapped at his hand. "No photos."

He rolled his eyes. "The photographers are still wandering around the park, but you can hide if you see one."

"Like she always does," Elizabeth said, giggling, putting her arm companionably through her twin's. "It's OK, Charlie. We'll turn our backs. We can *moon* them."

That made Charlie laugh.

"You two," Jonathan said, shaking his head tolerantly. "Come on, or Mom will be on the rampage."

"Thanks for showing us your trailer, Georgie,"

Charlie said. "I mean *caravan*. Can I talk to you about the other trailers you make? The fake ones?" Her eyes said that she wanted to talk about more than trailers.

"Charlotte!" Jonathan shook an admonishing finger. "They're not *fakes*. They're replicas, with some modern additions." He added for Georgie's benefit, "Sorry. My father will only restore originals."

"That's OK," Georgie assured him. "Charlie has already told me that…but it would probably be interesting for her to talk to our vintage restoration team and take a tour through the Elkhart facility next time she's in the area." She put her hand on Charlie's arm and gave a slight squeeze. "Your Dad might like to come to visit with you. But meanwhile, before you go today, make sure you find me, and I'll introduce you to Tammy. She's the person who handles most of the liaison for our vintage clients, whether they want to restore original trailers or order a modern replica."

She could feel Charlie's relief that they could continue their conversation later.

"I'd love it." Quickly, Charlie looked at Jonathan. "I'll come and serve morning tea and dodge the photographers if I can talk to Tammy after. Deal?"

"Women," he said easily. "Always bargaining. OK, squirt. Come and do the right thing, and then you can go and talk renovation until the sun goes down. Now, scoot!"

Charlie gave in. "I'll come and see you later, Georgie."

"Fine. If you can't see me, head for Tammy's trailer—the red one with the striped awning outside. There'll probably be a little white poodle there."

Jonathan grinned at her again, firmly marshaled his sisters, and herded them down the steps.

Georgie watched them walk away, her mind whirling.

Interesting family dynamics, she thought. The girls called their brother Jon and called each other Charlie and Beth, but Jonathan stuck to the formal versions of the girls' names: Charlotte and Elizabeth. She wouldn't mind betting that this was what Madelyn Draper preferred. She looked the type.

The girls seemed to be good pals; no resentment on Charlie's part about her much prettier twin. Jonathan, too, seemed to treat them alike.

And yet, Charlie didn't want him to know she was helping Ricky. *They always fought,* she'd said.

Hmm. Time to find Tammy and fill her in.

There were more questions she wanted to ask Charlie before she left for the day.

It was several hours before Charlie visited them again, which gave Georgie plenty of time to fill Tammy in on the real reason for the child's visit.

Tammy's eyes lit up, and she sat up in her chair, a move that elicited a sleepy whine of protest from the poodle in her lap. "Sorry, Trixxi. Go back to sleep." She patted her soothingly. "Does this mean another case for us?"

"Seems so," Georgie said, grinning at her. "Feeling the need to exercise those brain cells?"

"That, and it's just plain good fun making the bad guys pay," Tammy said, mulling over what Georgie had just told her. "Except for the court cases that go along with it all." She narrowed her eyes at Georgie. "You didn't tell us about *that* when you came up with the bright idea of the Crystal Ball Investigation Team."

Georgie wasn't going to argue with her. Court cases and the endless paperwork and talk to lawyers that went along with it *were* a pain. First, Jerry's abduction by a prepper who was more a criminal than a survivalist, and then Jaxx Saxby's stalker wreaking havoc just four months ago. They'd all had enough. And they were sick of the media coverage too.

"Maybe we should make it a condition of all future investigations," she suggested. "All work done undercover. No names, no pack drill."

"Sounds good in theory." Tammy re-tied the scarlet ribbon on Trixxi's topknot. It matched Tammy's bandana, which went with her cherry-sprigged 50s playsuit. Trixxi was clad in a doggie coat made of the same fabric, and the two of them had posed for about ten thousand photos that day. "Unfortunately, it required our testimony to put them away. Maybe this time we won't have to do police reports and what-not."

"Let's agree to make every effort," Georgie said feelingly. "Anonymous phone calls to the police, maybe?"

"Or let the family sort it out."

"If they'll listen." Georgie wasn't so sure about the Draper family when it came to their black-sheep son. "We were interrupted before I could ask Charlie more questions, but it sounds as though Mom is keeping Ricky at arm's length, although Dad might be a bit more malleable."

"That Madelyn makes me want to clench my teeth," Tammy said. "Something about her. Too perfect? Too smooth?" She pondered. "Too much the socialite, maybe. I like Douglas Draper, though. And I *love* his car and trailer. Our vintage reno team would enjoy talking with him about that."

"I Googled the family while I was waiting for you to finish posing for the cameras," Georgie told her. "I already knew a bit about them because they usually turn up to the big vintage rallies, but I found out more. Douglas Draper made his money in computer games—he's a massive geek, apparently, some kind of genius at designing games. Money's still rolling in hand over fist, and he spends some of it on his collection of vintage cars and trailers."

"I imagine Madelyn goes through the rest," Tammy said. "What does the Ken Doll do?"

"Jonathan? He's a bit more than a Ken doll. Have you met him face to face?"

"Yep," Tammy said. "He used his wiles on me and persuaded me to meet him later on for a drink. I thought: why not? Since Jerry had to stay back at Elkhart to walk the amazing Ms. Saxby through her equally amazing new motorhome."

"Oh," Georgie said. "I see." She eyed Tammy warily. "You and Jerry are OK, aren't you?" *Please don't split up with Jerry,* she thought. She wanted Tammy as a sister-in-law. But then, Jerry could be a real pain. After being his sister for the best part of thirty years, she should know.

"Oh, we're fine," Tammy said airily. "I just know that Jaxx is going to make every effort to seduce him while he's taking her for a test drive. I'm certain Jerry won't succumb, but just the thought of it makes me want to slam a few cupboard doors. Or..." she scratched Trixxi's stomach, "or go and have a drink with someone who is even more handsome than Jerry. And make sure that the photos go on Facebook."

"Anyway...where were we?" Georgie tracked the conversation back in her mind. "Jonathan... Ken doll...oh yeah, what does he do? He works for his dad. Not in programming, but management somewhere."

"Real management or jobs-for-the-family-type management?"

"Real management. He's got an MBA, so he's not stupid."

"And the black sheep?" Tammy inquired.

"That was the interesting part. He's into computer games too—logical, I guess, growing up as the son of Douglas Draper—but he's making money *playing* them. He buys and sells virtual real estate and characters. I had no idea you could do that. He builds up kingdoms and whatever and then sells his stake in a game and starts again. Kind of like flipping real estate, only it's all imaginary. Who would have thought?" She thought of the web pages she'd scrolled through and the members of the Draper family she'd met that morning. "I saw photos of him. He looks like his dad and Charlie." She craned her head and looked outside the trailer to make sure that Charlie wasn't within earshot since they were expecting her at any time. "It's like there's a line drawn down the middle of this family. There's Madelyn and Jonathan and Elizabeth, the beautiful people who have looks and money and fame. Then there's Dad, who has the fame and the money but missed out in the looks department. On that side, you also have Richard—Ricky—the eldest son and the one who's had a brush with the law, and Charlie, who is the homeliest of the lot until she smiles."

"And who doesn't get to be in the family photos," Tammy pointed out. "That's a bit cruel."

"I think that might be Charlie's own decision," Georgie said thoughtfully. "Poor girl's probably had a negative experience or two, given Madelyn's position socially. There'd be photos all the time."

Tammy, sitting opposite the door, was looking straight over at Madelyn's upmarket afternoon tea party. "I think I see Charlie breaking away from the group and heading here now. Is she wearing blue and white?"

"That's her."

"OK," Tammy said. "Showtime. Let's see what else we can find out, and then I'll do my bit later with the Ken doll."

CHAPTER 4

The Black Sheep

Georgie stuck her head around the door, watching Charlie's progress, and beckoned with a welcoming smile as soon as she caught her eye. "Over here, Charlie!"

Charlie looked behind her as though checking that nobody was following and hurried up to the door. The first thing she saw was Trixxi, lying blissfully comatose on Tammy's lap with her paws up in the air.

A wide grin split her face as she looked from the dog to Tammy. "I saw the two of you having your photos taken earlier!" She bounded up the steps and reached over to tickle Trixxi's tummy. "She's gorgeous." The dog snuffled and didn't move.

"That she is," Tammy agreed. "Our little mascot. Do you have dogs, Charlie?"

The smile died. "No, Mom doesn't like dogs."

"Well, then, you'll have to share Trixxi." Tammy wriggled across the seat to make more room. "Sit here." As soon as Charlie slid in beside her, she passed Trixxi across.

Good move, Georgie thought, giving the girl something to distract her while she told them what she was there for.

"Did you have something to eat or drink over at your Mom's afternoon tea, or were you too busy being the waitress?" Georgie asked.

An expression of mischief flickered in Charlie's eyes. "Beth and I sneaked our favorite cupcakes."

"Good." Tammy patted her on the arm. "That's a kid's job. Although Georgie tells me you're almost a teenager."

"Yes. In twelve days."

"Not yet thirteen," Tammy said, looking at her admiringly, "and already you know more about restoring vintage trailers than I do. Very impressive."

Charlie flushed with pleasure, and her wonderful smile transformed her face again. "I don't know *that* much. I just help out my Dad."

"I hope you can both come to Elkhart. Our reno team would love to talk with you."

"We will. I know he'll take me." She stroked Trixxi's topknot. "Won't he, Trixxi?"

Georgie, mindful that any of the Drapers might appear at any moment to whisk Charlie away again, decided to cut to the chase. "Charlie, I've told Tammy everything we've discussed so far. We kind of have a private investigation team going here, and we have solved quite a few little mysteries." She put a finger to her lips and said in an exaggerated whisper, looking around as though being wary of eavesdroppers, "but don't tell anyone. We don't make it public."

Charlie's eyes widened. "I know about the Jaxx Saxby stalker. You mean *you* figured that out?"

Georgie nodded. "Regrettably, not before she did some damage, but it could have been worse." She opened the notepad in front of her and picked up a pen. "Let's start by getting your brother's contact details, just in case you have to leave quickly. And while I think of it, can you phone him and tell him we'd like to see him?"

Charlie nodded and recited her brother's phone number and address, watching Georgie write it down.

"OK." Georgie sat back and gave Charlie her full attention. "Now, tell us everything you think we should know."

Charlie took a deep breath and began. It was a sad tale of an elder son who had gone off the rails as a teenager—which was when illegal substances and a swathe of questionable friends had entered the picture—and had then appeared to reform in his early twenties, only to fall from grace a few months ago when he stole and hocked his mother's jewelry.

They listened closely, asking a few questions along the way, until Charlie finally ran out of steam. "He didn't do it," she ended forcefully. "He says he didn't, and I believe him."

"Don't take this the wrong way, Charlie," Georgie said. "You know that I sensed he was innocent in the reading, right? But I have to ask —*why* do you believe him? What makes you think he couldn't have done it?"

She was silent for a moment and then formed her hand into a fist and thumped herself on the chest, over her heart. "I just feel it *here*. Because I know him. He admits to some of the stuff he did when he was younger—but not this. Mom even told him just to own up, and he could come to visit again and be part of the family, and he said no. He wasn't going to put his hand up for something he didn't do."

Georgie, watching her face, could see that she

believed it with all her heart and soul. "Were you two close when he lived at home?"

"Yes. Even when he was fighting with Mom and Dad, seeing all those friends they didn't like, he'd still hang out sometimes with Beth and me. We were only about four, and he'd come and play tea-parties and dress-ups." Charlie gave a slight smile at the memory. "Sometimes we used to put Mom's old makeup on him. Or we'd dress him up as the Prince."

That didn't sound like a boy who rejected his family for his peer group, Georgie thought. "Did Jonathan join in too?"

"No. He and Ricky didn't get on."

"What about when he was older, when you started school?"

"Oh, yes." Charlie nodded, her eyes shining at the memory. "Ricky used to put on these great games afternoons for Beth and me, with some of his friends. He likes to design worlds, you see, and he'd play different games to see what we liked."

"I read about Ricky," Georgie told her. "He's a very successful player, I believe."

"Yes. Mom thinks he should get a degree in computer programming and have a proper career, like Jon, but Ricky says he'd rather play games than code them." The light left Charlie's eyes. "And then the jewelry went missing, and it turned up at the pawnshop, and Ricky got the blame. Now Mom's furious and says she's not letting him in the house until he turns over a new leaf, and Dad just gets sad and won't talk about him, and Ricky hardly ever even phones me." Her dark brows drew together in the ferocious frown that Jonathan had admonished her about earlier, making her homely little face even plainer.

Georgie felt like putting her arms around the girl and giving her an all-enveloping hug but knew instinctively that this wasn't what Charlie wanted. She needed someone to make things right again, to bring her adored older brother back home. To clear his name.

"Charlie, we'll help as much as we can. But if it wasn't Ricky, who else do you think it might have been? Any ideas?"

"It has to have been someone who knows our house. That's what the police said. But Mom has friends there all the time, and fund-raising groups meet there. Jon brings friends around. My cousin Tyler visits all the time." Her lip jutted as she said his name. "Tyler's mean. He pretends to be friendly, but I've heard him talk about me to Jon's friends." She ducked her head and got busy playing with the ribbon in Trixxi's topknot, but not before Georgie saw the flash of hurt in her eyes.

She could imagine the kinds of things Tyler had been saying.

With a direct line of sight to Madelyn Draper's afternoon tea party, Tammy gave them a heads-up. "Looks like your brother and sister are heading this way. We'd better start talking about vintage renovations." She slid a stack of pamphlets advertising vintage trailers to the center of the table and swiftly opened up a couple of them, so they were looking at photos of interiors. "Do you have a cell phone, Charlie?"

"Yes." Georgie scribbled down the number dictated by Charlie and then dug into her pocket for the business cards she always kept there. She passed one to the girl. "Here. Keep this. I'll text you if I need to talk, OK? And we'll see Ricky as soon as we can."

"Thank you. Thank you so much!"

"No guarantees," Georgie warned her gently. "We'll do what we can, though."

"He didn't do it. You'll see when you meet him. I'll phone him as soon as I can, tell him to see you." Sitting on the same side as Tammy, Charlie could see her brother and sister coming closer. She waved and then pulled one of the pamphlets to her, being careful not to disturb Trixxi too much. One of the photos caught her attention, and she pointed. "You know, this looks so much like one that Dad and I worked on last year. Did your team do this?"

"No, it's one of our modernized replicas. We always consult with our reno team, but they don't work on them." Warming to her favorite subject, Tammy found another pamphlet. "Look at this one. The cupboard design was their idea. Have you ever worked on an Airstream?"

"No, but we went to see one that his friend had." Charlie launched into a discussion with Tammy, and when Beth and Jonathan appeared at the door a few seconds later, there was no hint that they had been discussing the fate of their black sheep brother.

Georgie was intrigued by the dynamics of the Draper family. She was keen to meet not only Ricky but his parents Madelyn and Douglas.

Tammy was seeing Jonathan later…maybe she could finagle an invitation to the Draper household.

CHAPTER 5

The Son and Heir

There were plenty of envious glances thrown Tammy's way when Jonathan Draper headed her way.

She had been aware of Jonathan's eyes on her throughout the afternoon, especially when she and three of the others bounced up for an energetic jive to *Chantilly Lace* but ignored him. If Jonathan Draper were the type she suspected, he'd treat indifference as a challenge.

Sure enough, at a few minutes before six, he was tapping her on the shoulder. "Hey, Tammy. Still want to meet up for that drink?"

She feigned surprise, glancing at her Paul Ditisheim retro rose gold watch. "Jonathan! Is it that time already?" She tilted her head, looking up with a dazzling smile.

He treated her to an equally impressive lady-killer grin, which made his dimples form two deep grooves in his cheeks, and out of the corner of her eye, she could see several of her female friends take on a glazed expression as they gazed at him. "No hurry," he said. "You look like you're all having a good time."

"I am, but I've been waiting all day for the chance to see inside that Shasta of your father's!" She jumped up. "We can come back and join the group later."

The chairs and tables set up around the Draper's trailer were mainly empty, except for Douglas Draper and a few of his cronies drinking beer and exchanging renovation stories. Madelyn had taken her twin daughters home, apparently, to prepare for the next day's garden party and tour of the Draper collection of vintage cars and trailers.

One of the men sitting with Jonathan's dad, with white hair and a cheerful wrinkled face, tipped his bottle in her direction. "Hi, Tammy!"

She moved across and planted a kiss on his cheek. "Hi, Chuck! Ready to buy a trailer from me yet?" She winked. It was a well-worn joke between them; like Douglas Draper, Chuck James was obsessed with authentic renovation.

"That modern rubbish? Not a chance in hell,"

he said with mock scorn. "You and young Jerry can try until the cows come home, but you won't get me in one." In an aside to Douglas, he said, "Tammy runs the vintage trailer division at Johnny B. Goode."

"Well, Jerry runs it," she corrected him and sent a laughing glance at Jonathan. "But of course, I'm the real power behind the throne."

Chuck looked from her to Jonathan, speculation in his eyes. "Jerry not here?"

"No. He's off on a road trip with Jaxx Saxby in her new motorhome," she said truthfully, knowing that her words could be interpreted in several different ways, and deliberately changed the subject before they could elicit the information that it was a test run. "Jerry likes motorhomes; I love vintage." She beamed at Douglas Draper. "You've done a fine job restoring this trailer. And the Chevy. I don't dare ask how many man-hours you put in."

"It wasn't just me," he admitted, although his face was glowing with pride. "I have some talented friends." He smiled at her, and the laughter lines around his eyes deepened. Like Charlie, his homely face lit up when he smiled. Strong genes, Tammy thought: Charlie was a miniature version of her dad, although her features were a little more irregular.

"If you think this is nice," the third man said, "you should see his '53 Airfloat Navigator. That's my wife's favorite."

"I know that trailer," Tammy said, nodding. "We used elements of that design in our new hybrid." She clapped her hands to her cheeks theatrically. "Oh no, did I just say 'new' and 'hybrid' in the same breath while talking to restoration experts?"

They all laughed, and then Douglas Draper said the words she'd been hoping to hear. "Madelyn has organized some kind of party thing tomorrow for some of the vintage crowd. You're invited to come and see my collection if you'd care to ?"

"Thank you! I'd love it." Tammy dimpled at him. "I'll wear a disguise, so nobody knows that the enemy has infiltrated."

They all laughed, as she had planned. "Kicks off at around eleven," Douglas told her. "You'll be very welcome."

Jonathan interrupted with mock impatience. "All right, that's enough vintage talk for now! Time for a relaxed drink."

"Enough vintage talk?" Tammy gave him a playful punch. "That's it, then. You go back to the party. I'll stay here and talk to your dad."

The older men laughed again at Jonathan's

expense, and then Tammy let him usher her into the Shasta. As she expected, it was beautifully restored. Jonathan patiently let her ooh and aah and ask questions for ten minutes, and then sat her down with champagne in a fluted glass.

Tammy caught a glimpse of the label on the bottle. Yikes. Nothing but the best for the Draper family.

She toasted Jonathan. "Here's to the world of vintage trailers."

He clinked glasses. "And automobiles. You grow up in my house, and it's about cars first, trailers second. Mom's the one more into trailers. She can play dress-up and enjoy the social scene."

"The roles seem to be fairly evenly divided among your family," Tammy said, conscious of his eyes on her lips as she sipped, the bubbles tickling her nose. "Your Mom and Beth like to dress up and enjoy the retro lifestyle, don't they? Whereas Charlie says she helps your dad with the restoration work."

"You've nailed it. Elizabeth is a born fashionista. And Charlotte? She's always trailed about after Dad with her own toolset. Only now, they're grown-up tools, not toys."

"And you work in the business too, don't you?"

Tammy said. "The Drapers remind me a bit of the Goode family. Everyone involved in some way."

He shrugged. "Well, we all enjoy it. As you'll see when you visit tomorrow."

No mention of the missing elder brother, Tammy noted—and she didn't want to send up a flag by mentioning Ricky.

She went about it in a roundabout way. "I've seen you around at some of the vintage rallies. Mostly the ones that focus on automobiles now that I come to think of it." Tilting her head, she raised an eyebrow at him. "You were never tempted to restore vintage cars? Buy? Sell? Anything?"

"I admire them. Same as I admire a painstakingly restored trailer," he said. His eyes swept over her. "Not to mention the women that decorate them and live in them." He laughed, a pleasant bass chuckle. "I know, I know, that sounds like a line. But you've got to admit; there's something to be said for fifties fashion." He looked wryly down at his outfit. "Even this."

"In other words," Tammy teased, "you're just like your mother and sister. You like looking at them and playing with them, but not doing the work."

"Got me. I'm the general manager of Dad's company."

"Do you enjoy business?"

"Not particularly," he said frankly. "I found the MBA easy, and it kept my parents happy. Dad's easy to work with, and he'd rather design games or pull on a pair of overalls to work on a rusty old car than spend hours on management tasks." He spread his hands wide. "Hence, the son and heir gets the job."

The son and heir? Ricky didn't even rate a mention, even though he was the eldest son?

She left it alone and let the conversation flow naturally. "I guess I do a bit of both: managing the division and working in it. Not restoration." She treated him to a display of her dimples. "I work with the engineers on translating features of various vintage trailers into modern equivalents. But I get to work with the design team and Georgie's road team and kick up my heels with the vintage crowd at rallies. It's a good life."

He nodded, and she could tell from the small intake of breath and a slight narrowing of his eyes that he was going to change tack.

"I thought you and Jerry Goode had a 'thing' going." He made quotation marks with his fingers. "That's what I heard in vintage circles. I asked about you."

Tammy shrugged casually. "We were together for a while." She mentally apologized to Jerry, then at the same time remembered where he was and who he was with, and told herself to forget feeling guilty. "He's off with Jaxx Saxby now. She had her eye on him from the start. And well, if you've seen Jaxx…"

"I've seen Jaxx. I'd imagine half the country knows who she is after the stalking story made the news. But…" he sat back and this time, gave her a more thorough appraisal. "She's a little obvious, don't you think? You - well, you're more like the women in my family. Beautiful and classy."

"Why Jonathan," she mocked, "next you'll be asking me to marry you."

He gave a crack of laughter. "Could do worse. But let's take it slowly, shall we? Tomorrow is a good starting point. Come see the Draper hacienda."

Hacienda indeed, she thought. Fifty-room mansion, more like. With purpose-built garages to house the vintage automobiles and trailers.

But he had a point. Take it slowly, and when he was relaxed, she'd slip in a few more questions.

The son and heir, indeed.

She hadn't met him yet, but she was already feeling sorry for Richard Draper, eldest son and a sheep so black that nobody mentioned his name.

CHAPTER 6

20s Style

The following day, Georgie had three phone calls in a row. The first was from Layla, the missing member of her road team, apologizing for not making it to Boulder for the first day of the rally after car problems.

"I'll be there by lunchtime," she assured Georgie. "But I'm betting we won't sell many of our kind of vintage trailers. It's all about restoration at the Draper meet, isn't it?"

"Mostly," Georgie agreed. "We usually snare a few new customers who want the look and the fun without the work. But that's not why you want to get here ASAP. We have another case."

"We do? Cool!"

"Tell you about it when you get here," Georgie said as her phone dinged. "I've got a call waiting.

See you this afternoon." She switched to the second caller, her heart warming. Scott. Two more days, and he'd be with her again. "Hey," she greeted him. "How's life in Montana?"

"Full of trees and hikers who don't want to obey the rules," he said. "I've earned my money on this stint, let me tell you. I've got a humdinger of a black eye."

"No!"

"Drunken hunter took a swing at me."

Georgie frowned. "Are you OK?"

"A shiner never killed anyone," he said laconically. "Now he's in the lockup for his efforts, and I finally have a month off. How's the rally?"

"Fun, but there's other news. Would you believe we've got a new case?"

"We have?" Interest quickened in his voice. "It's been a while. I was beginning to think you'd lost your touch."

"So was I," she admitted. "But I was glad to have a rest." She filled him in on Charlie's visit, Ricky's problems, and Tammy's pending visit to the Draper residence to do some more digging. "I plan to phone Ricky Draper this morning and arrange a visit. I have no idea how receptive he'll be. This is all little Charlie's idea."

"Am I allowed to say be careful, or is that patronizing?"

"You never patronize me," Georgie said, smiling. "And yes, I'll be careful. Will you still get here tomorrow? I plan to stay around for a week or so."

"I'll probably be there in time for supper unless I make better time than I think."

They talked for a few more minutes, with Scott going into more detail about life as a Montana park ranger, until the third call came in.

Georgie sighed. "I'm popular this morning. Gotta go, Scott."

"Don't forget: take care. Love you."

"Love you too. See you soon." Georgie felt the same fleeting regret that she always felt at having to hang up on the man in her life when he was working in another state but was soon distracted by the pleasant baritone voice on the other end of the phone.

"Georgie Goode?"

"Yes." She didn't recognize the voice. "Can I help you?"

"My little sister Charlie seems to think so," said the voice. "She told me I had to phone you. Pinkie promise. You know how serious that is."

That made her laugh. "I do indeed. I guess you're Ricky?"

"Yes." The voice grew more guarded. "According to Charlie, she's told you *everything*, which is a bit alarming. Quite honestly, I have no idea what she thinks you'll be able to do about it all. She says you're a gypsy fortune-teller…?"

Georgie groaned. She couldn't help it. "And you think you have to see some flaky psychic because you promised your baby sister. Tell you what, Ricky. Let's just meet, and you can make up your own mind."

"No offense, but I haven't much choice. Charlie is the one bright spot in my life right now. I can't disappoint her."

"Fine." Georgie didn't plan to waste her breath convincing him. "Where and when?"

"My place, I guess? Anytime is fine; I work from home."

"Let's make it eleven, then. Charlie gave me the address."

"See you then." With that, he ended the call.

Not too bad, Georgie thought. While Tammy was invading the Draper garden party, charming the golden boy of the family and staying alert for any tidbits of information, she would be knocking on the door of the black sheep. By the time Layla and Scott arrived to join the think tank, they should be starting to put the pieces together.

Before she dressed for the Draper garden party, Tammy spent some time on the Internet, skimming old newspaper articles about the Drapers and scrolling through Facebook pages. Douglas Draper had six vintage cars and five trailers on his property, all housed in secure garages and insured up to the hilt. One of his personal favorites was his 1922 Mercer Series 5 Raceabout. Decision made: 1920s fashion it would be.

Satisfied, she closed her laptop and went out to her car to unearth her backup wardrobe: Tammy never traveled anywhere without a selection of vintage clothes, and she loved the long, elegant lines of her 20s outfits. Some she bought: some she ran up on her sewing machine; replicas of outfits she'd seen in photos.

She found the one she was looking for: the white crepe afternoon dress with the velvet let-in that she'd made the previous summer. All it needed was a single strand of pearls (very expensive: just let Madelyn try biting those) and the right hairstyle. Tammy knew how to create perfect finger waves with her vintage wave clamp. She was now an expert at rolling her hair under to mimic the era's popular cropped hairdos.

Forty-five minutes later, she was ready; Cupid's bow lips and gray smudged eye shadow completing the look. *OK, Jonathan*, she thought. *Here I come.*

The Draper access road was long and wide and seemed to go on forever before Tammy reached the house. She cruised into a circular driveway and parked her car at the end of a line of others in an immaculately raked gravel parking lot to the side of an extended garage divided into separate bays. All of the security roller doors were open, revealing the gleaming classic cars inside. Behind it was a similar building with the vintage trailers on show. Tammy counted ten bays in each garage. Douglas Draper had plans to add a few more to his collection.

Already, people were wandering around admiring the vehicles and gathering in clusters to talk. Most were dressed for the occasion in vintage clothes, and she wasn't the only one in 20s fashion. Tammy would love to have joined them and drooled over the trailers, but she had a job to do. She slipped the car keys and phone into a slim beaded clutch and looked around for one of her hosts.

Jonathan was already heading her way. The look of a 20s owner of a speakeasy suited him down to the ground. No doubt any look suited him: a living, breathing Ken doll, except a lot more animated and with charm and humor as part of the package.

"Tammy!" He tilted his head to one side as he admired her. "Perfect. We're a pair."

"Couldn't have done it better if we'd planned it," she agreed.

"Refreshments first or a tour of Dad's vintage goodies?" A wry smile lit his face. "Or need I ask?"

"I've been hankering to see the 1922 Race-about," Tammy admitted, giving him the complete wide-eyed treatment along with a perfect 20s pout. "That's what inspired the outfit. I *have* to have a photo of myself with it. Maybe Santa will bring me one for Christmas."

They both laughed. Since the Raceabout was worth around three hundred and fifty grand, *that* wasn't likely to happen any time soon, but it was nice to dream.

"Come on, then." Jonathan took her free hand and led her toward the vintage cars, chatting comfortably about his father's collection. Smooth, thought Tammy, feeling his warm fingers close around her own. Flirting with women came as easily as breathing to Jonathan Draper.

They went directly to the Raceabout bay, and Tammy huffed out a sigh of delight. It really was a thing of beauty. She walked around it, itching to run her fingers over the glowing caramel paintwork and rich black leather seats. "It's gorgeous."

"It's OK to touch it," Jonathan said, reading her mind. "Gives Dad an excuse to come out and buff them all up again after his cronies leave."

Tammy didn't need a second invitation. She leaned over and looked at the dials. "Fast little baby in its day, wasn't it?"

"One of the speediest sports cars of its era," came Douglas Draper's voice from behind her. "75 miles an hour or better."

She straightened up and beamed at him as he regarded the Raceabout with the expression of a doting parent. "It's beautiful."

"It's one of my favorites." He cast a rueful glance at the side panels. "Not as easy to jump in and out it these days, without any doors. Madelyn prefers the others."

"Would you mind taking a photo of me standing next to it?"

He laughed. "I spend a good part of any open

day taking photos of people with the cars. Or in them. Want to hop in?"

Tammy glanced down at her dress, a slim sheath extending to mid-calf. Unless she hiked it up around her waist, she had no hope of climbing into the Raceabout. "Uh…"

"Allow me." Without waiting for permission, Jonathan picked her up and swung her over the side. Tammy let out an involuntary squeal, clutching on to his arms, but Jonathan did it as easily as though she weighed half as much.

"Hold it!" another voice called, and there was a series of flashes as a photographer captured the moment while Jonathan settled her into the passenger seat.

Jonathan walked around and vaulted into the driver's seat, grinning at her while he adjusted his hat. "There. A 20s couple out for a drive." He held out his hand. "Camera?"

"It's just my phone." She snapped open the clutch, activated her camera phone, and handed it to Jonathan, who passed it to his father. "Thanks."

The photographer circled the car, snapping away. "Perfect. Perfect! This will make a great post. Can you two play to the camera for me?" He popped his head out from behind his Nikon and addressed Tammy. "Sorry, what's your name?"

"Tammy."

"Let's have an iconic 20s pout, Tammy. Then lots of grins, laughter, good-time girl, you know…"

Tammy did as he asked, with Jonathan readily joining in. His father took a few pictures on her phone and then just stood watching, proud of his car and his handsome son.

It was right then that Madelyn arrived.

Tammy, her attention caught by the flash of white at Douglas's elbow, glanced up, and her grin died.

Oh no.

They were wearing the same dress, except Tammy's was a knockoff, and Madelyn's was, no doubt, a hugely expensive original. Judging by the glint in Madelyn's eye and her tight smile, she was livid.

Then the photographer clicked again, and there was a flash. "Iconic shot," he said with a grin. "Two women in the same dress."

For a nanosecond, Tammy could have sworn that Madelyn actually snarled.

CHAPTER 7

Ricky Draper

Fourteen miles away, Georgie knocked on the door of the converted train carriage that was Ricky Draper's home and then stood back and waited.

Footsteps sounded on the other side of the door, and it swung open to reveal a younger version of Douglas Draper, right down to the slightly protruding ears, clear gray eyes, and potato nose.

He smiled politely and stepped back. "Hi, Georgie. Come on in."

"Hi, Ricky." She was already predisposed to like him because of Charlie, but there was something else. The moment their eyes met, she felt instantly in tune with him, almost as though he were an old friend.

He seemed to feel it, too, his forehead creasing slightly as he stared at her.

Bizarre. That had never happened before, not even with Scott.

She stepped inside, intrigued. The front half of the carriage appeared to be a combined living room and office. A door on the side wall was open, revealing a sunny indoor/outdoor area at the side, filled with pot plants and cane chairs with cheerful splashy covers in primary colors. Ricky had two separate work tables set up side-by-side, one with two large monitors and a laptop perched on a stand with a separate keyboard. There was a second laptop on the other table, along with notepads and pencils and a range of 3D action figures, lined up along the back of the desk like soldiers.

In front of a large-screen TV mounted on the wall, he had arranged a small sofa and a couple of easy chairs, and there was some kind of game console resting on a coffee table.

Everything was compact. There wasn't much room to move around, but it all worked.

"This is just like living in a trailer," Georgie said. "Except you have a lot more room than I do."

"Not a lot of difference," he agreed. "I always loved Dad's vintage trailers. Maybe that's why I was sold on this when it came up as a rental." He nodded at the easy chairs and then to the outside area. "Inside or outside?"

"Outside," she decided.

"Go take a seat. I'll get us some drinks. Tea, coffee, soda…?"

"I drink them all," Georgie told him. "Surprise me."

He disappeared through a door at the end of the room into a small corridor, and Georgie heard his footsteps moving down towards the end of the carriage. She went through to the neighboring area, found a sunny spot at a circular breakfast table near an open shutter, and set the bag containing her crystal ball down beside her.

This case was intriguing her more and more. Her first reading with Charlie had left her with the unmistakable sense that Ricky was innocent of the crime that had split the family, and now that she had come face to face with him, she was even more confident.

That, she decided, was one of the side benefits of having the Sight. Often it could be vague or frustrating or present her with clues in obscure images or riddles—but when she felt this sure about something, she was never wrong.

If Richard Draper hadn't stolen his mother's jewelry, then who had - and why?

When he returned with a tray containing a pitcher of home-made lemonade and tall frosted glasses, Ricky set it down on the table, sat opposite her, and got straight to the point.

"I Googled you," he told her. "Naturally."

"Naturally." She grinned at him. "I did the same for you. So what did you find?"

"Thousands of hits. You've been in the public eye for years as part of the Johnny B. Goode RV Empire. Over the past twelve months or so, there's been more about your gypsy trailer and a couple of court cases. From what I read, I gather you are some kind of psychic detective."

"Really?" Georgie was startled. "Is that the impression you're getting?"

"That's what a couple of reporters have said. There was a lot on the Jaxx Saxby page. Says you gave her the idea for her new cable TV series."

Georgie groaned. "She's been after me to join her for months. I keep saying no, but Jaxx doesn't give up easily."

"Anyway," he went on, "I'm getting nowhere fast trying to prove my innocence, so you might as well have a go." He immediately winced. "Sorry, that sounded as though you're the last resort, didn't it?"

Georgie waved his apology aside. "Heard it all before."

"What, exactly, did Charlie tell you?"

She told him as much as she could remember, watching the expressions play out on his face: sadness, residual anger, and resignation. When she finished, he just nodded, picked up a glass, and took a long draught of lemonade while marshaling his thoughts.

"I can tell you my side of it, or you can just do your thing," he said at last. "What works best for you? Will my take on the situation muddy the waters?"

Georgie thought about that for a moment. He was being entirely fair, not trying to influence her at all. Why not run with that?

"Crystal ball," she decided. "I'll tell you what I get—if anything—and you can put in your two cents as we go."

"Sounds good." He watched while she pulled the crystal ball out of her bag, unwrapped it, and set it on the table, moving the lemonade to one side.

"Just focus on the problem," she advised him. "I'll tell you if some information starts coming through."

Mostly, she approached a reading with a philosophical attitude: maybe she'd get something, maybe she wouldn't. This time, oddly, she did not doubt that she would get a hit. Her fingers tingled the moment she touched the crystal ball, and her pulse fluttered.

A mist began to swirl in the crystalline depths, and immediately, faces began to form. She recognized all of them: the Draper family. Intact, with the two older brothers and the twin girls, with Madelyn and Douglas standing behind their children. The kids were all younger: the girls looked about seven or eight; Jonathan a handsome teenager, Ricky a frowning young man of maybe…twenty?

The difficult years she'd heard about, she would guess.

Georgie peered closer. They were all at some kind of vintage rally, standing in front of a shining black classic car.

"I can see a classic car of some kind," she said. "You're all standing beside it. It's black, kind of boxy-looking. You know, like one of those old T-model Fords."

"Dad's 1912 Rolls Royce Silver Ghost," he said immediately. "Beautiful ride. Lovely touring car." He got up and went into the next room and came back with a photo. "That was the last rally I went to. After that, it all became too difficult." He handed it to her, and she was looking at a photographic representation of the scene in the crystal ball.

"Wow." She glanced from the photo to the crystal ball, but already the images were dissolving. "What do you mean, it all became too difficult?"

"Too many people knew about my teenage idiocy. Someone came up to her there and asked if I was through my 'difficult period' or still causing problems. Incredibly embarrassing, according to my mother. Better if I stayed away."

Georgie stared thoughtfully at the photo. She could have torn it down the middle and had half of the family in each hand. On one side, you had Douglas, Ricky, and Charlie, all with the same homely features. On the other, beaming at the camera, stood Beth, Jonathan, and Madelyn, all three blonde and gorgeous. The two girls were arm in arm, as different as night and day.

Ricky read her mind. "Like yin and yang, isn't it? Those who were first in line when good looks and charm were given out, and the others who were standing behind the door."

Georgie didn't bother with tactful denials. Life was what it was, and it was usually more challenging for those who looked a bit different. "Does it worry Charlie?"

"It didn't matter when she was small. Now she avoids photos. Says she hates the posing—which she does—but she's heard enough comments to make her sensitive about it." His forehead creased in a frown that was uncannily like his little sister's. "My mother is quite happy that she's taken that stance. She never said anything, but now every photo is a perfect photo. Madelyn, Jonathan, and Elizabeth. Dad's allowed to be in the odd photo; he has character and credibility, and he's loaded." He smiled without humor. "My words, not Mom's, but accurate enough."

"The twins seem to get on well."

"They do. Beth has Mom's looks and Dad's nature. Both girls are great kids, and I'm sure that Beth will always stick up for her sister. And I have a soft spot for Charlie, as you can imagine."

Georgie put down the photo and glanced back at the crystal ball, then instinctively jerked in surprise. This seemed to be a day for faces. The Draper family had been replaced by a young man with silvery fair hair. Late teens or early twenties, she'd guess. He was watching a girl approach. She grew larger and larger, emerging from the misty depths in the crystal ball until she reached the male. They grinned at each other, and Georgie shivered.

These two were not good news.

She glanced up. Ricky's eyes were on the crystal ball, but his face was blank.

"Can you see anything?" she asked.

"No. Should I be able to?"

"Not necessarily. Some can; some can't." She was a little surprised; she'd thought with the instant sense of connection that she'd had with Ricky, he'd be able to see what she could. "Can you see a mist?"

"No."

"It doesn't matter." It would have been easier, she thought, if he could see the same images she could. "I'm seeing a male and female, silvery blond hair, both good-looking. Maybe twentyish? Could be a few years either way."

"Alexis and Tyler," he provided. "My cousins. Mom's sister's kids."

"Do you get on with them?"

"On the surface," he said, but his eyes were cool. "They have always preferred Jonathan. They're around his age."

"OK." She watched while the cousins gradually faded from sight, but no more images were forthcoming. Something was nagging at her mind, though: something about a man.

A man with a black cat?

She glanced up at Ricky. "Do you know anyone with a cat?"

"I know lots of people with cats. And dogs. What kind of person? Young? Old?"

"All I know is that it's a man." Georgie shrugged. "That's what it's like for me, Ricky. Sometimes things are clear, but mostly they're not. I usually find it's like putting together a jigsaw puzzle —with most of the pieces so faded that you can't see them properly."

"That pretty much sums up what it's been like for me trying to figure this out," he said wryly.

Georgie dismissed the man with the cat for the moment and sat back, leaving her fingers resting on the crystal ball. "Why don't you tell me exactly what happened?"

CHAPTER 8

An Icy Future

Ricky started by sketching in a few details of his teenage years. It was all pretty much as Charlie had explained, but from the perspective of a man who regretted his rebellious youth. He'd flirted with drugs and had run with a wild crowd, most of whom both of his parents hated.

"Dad was the one who made me feel worst," he said. "He's such a good guy; he made me feel that I was letting him down. He hates drugs with a passion—any kind. Mom was just permanently angry and disgusted and mostly wouldn't talk to me."

"And Jonathan?"

"Jonathan never let an opportunity go by without twisting the knife," he said unemotionally. "He's always been the same. When we were kids, he'd set things up so that I looked like the bad guy, persecuting my little brother. Always went running to Mom."

Georgie thought of Jerry, who'd been a master of the same thing when they were children. He seemed to have improved a lot since meeting Tammy. Still, she could sympathize.

"When I started smoking weed, Jonathan didn't have to work so hard to discredit me," Ricky went on. "I did his job for him." He drummed his fingers on the table and then said, "Now, the jewelry."

Conscious of the crystal ball under her fingertips, Georgie left herself open to random thoughts, but nothing was coming through yet. "Go on."

"I was set up. Who or why is the question. I'd guess Jonathan because he was always open to widening the family rift, but he was with the rest of the family on the other side of the country when it happened. To cut a long story short, I got a phone call in response to an eBay ad I'd placed to sell part of my gaming collection. A 1990 Nintendo World Championships Gray Edition. I have two of them."

Georgie nodded, watching his face.

"I went to Mom and Dad's house to pick it up; all my duplicates are in the basement. It's a big collection." He waved a hand to encompass his railway carriage home. "No room here, as you can imagine. Anyway, I turned up at the address the guy provided and found an old lady living there who knew nothing about it. So I just took it home and waited for the buyer to phone; thought I must have written down the wrong address."

She stole a glance at the crystal ball, but couldn't see anything, so she returned her attention to Ricky.

"A few days later, Dad turned up at my door. They got home from the rally to find Mom's jewelry missing. They reported it to the police, but there was no evidence of anyone breaking in, and the jewelry turned up at a pawnshop in the next county. The manager isn't required to give details about where it came from, but Mom had photos and details, so she got it all back."

"So why did they suspect you? Because you were at the house?"

"Security records showed that the key code had been entered, and the video cameras showed me going in and out, carrying a box."

"The computer game."

"Yes, but it could have been anything…and the jewelry could have been inside the box too."

"Isn't that all circumstantial?"

"You'd think so. But the pawnshop was one that I used as a teenager, when I hocked my guitar and skis and a few other things for drug money, once Mom and Dad cut my allowance."

"But surely the manager would tell them it wasn't you?"

"He refused to give any information at all. Clearly, someone got to him. Mom and Dad didn't want any scandal, so they hushed it up and told the police it was a family misunderstanding. But they *know* it was me." He drew quote marks in the air with his fingers for the "know".

Georgie thought it through. "But I hear you're doing well buying and selling virtual real estate—or something like that—in computer games, and you have a valuable collection of vintage games as well. Why would you need to hock jewelry?"

"Why indeed?" The frustration in his voice grew. "That's what I pointed out to Mom and Dad, but once you've run with the wrong crowd… it's hard to prove you've changed."

"Motive," she said thoughtfully. "Why would someone frame you?"

The crystal ball was still giving her nothing, so she took her hands away. "Do you suspect anyone?"

"As I said, I would have said it was Jonathan, but he was nowhere near the place. Of course, he could have set up the phone call. But who broke in and took the jewelry? Who took it to the pawnbroker?"

Georgie stared at him with a frown, thinking. "And someone who knows that you sell vintage games on eBay? *And* that you keep your duplicates in the house."

He gave a grim nod. "My thoughts exactly. It narrows it down—family or friends or acquaintances of theirs that know enough to ask the right questions. I've had five months to think about this. I just keep going around in circles. But the jewelry's not the only thing."

At his words, Georgie sat back and waited. There was *more?*

"I was damn lucky not to end up in prison," he said. "The week after all that, I went out to pick up another collectible from a friend who's into the same thing. It was a Wednesday night, when I usually meet up with a group of gamers. Top-level guys, a mix of players and coders. This Wednesday, we'd called it off because there was a 48-hour gaming marathon online. All of which meant that instead of being out until midnight, as usual, I was away only for an hour or so."

Georgie guessed what he was going to say before he said it. "You disturbed an intruder?"

He nodded. "I saw lights on as soon as I turned

into the driveway. He shot out the back door and got away; there was a car waiting a few doors down. The lookout, I assume."

Instinctively, Georgie reached for the crystal ball. Nothing there, but she laid her hands on it anyway. "Did they take anything?"

"That was my first thought. I have the most valuable part of my collection here. But no, it was all intact. Nothing else appeared to be missing, either, when I did a quick search. I checked the computer, but it hadn't been turned on, so it didn't seem likely to be anyone after information about my virtual real estate or characters. Anyway, in the circles I move in, they'd be more likely to hack it, not break in."

He paused for a moment and looked at her keenly. "Just out of interest, let's see if you come up with the same conclusion I did. If they didn't break in to steal something, and assuming I hadn't arrived home before they had a chance to get what they wanted, then what was the motive?"

She saw it immediately. "To plant something."

"That's what I thought. And given my record as a teenager, what would they plant?"

"My God," she said. "Did you find anything?"

"Ice," he said. "In the freezer, along with the

real ice. Behind the ice cream. It took me over an hour to find it."

A shiver went up Georgie's spine. "What did you do?"

"Drove off like a bat out of hell to the outskirts of town and buried it under a billboard. *After* wiping the bag to make sure my fingerprints weren't on it. As far as I know, it's still there."

From the bleak look in his eyes, Georgie knew there was more coming.

"The drug squad turned up at around 3 am. Dogs and all. There was nothing to find, of course —but they trashed the place looking when it wasn't in the first place they tried."

"The freezer."

"Whoever it was," he said, "they knew enough to plant a set of scales and zip-lock bags in a kitchen drawer. I missed those."

Speechless, Georgie stared at him. Who hated Ricky enough to do this?

"After that," he said, "I installed new locks, security camera, the works. Cost me a fortune, but at least I can sleep at night. If I'd been busted for drugs, it would have destroyed my relationship with Dad."

"And your mother?"

"Already beyond repair," he said tightly. "Thanks to Jonathan and those teen years."

Georgie glanced again at the crystal ball, but there was nothing to see. She felt helpless. If Ricky had been mulling over this for five months and had come up with nothing but a vague suspicion that it might be Jonathan, how could she hope to find out who it was?

No, she decided, she couldn't think that way. *Wouldn't* think that way. Other cases had looked impossible to solve, too, until the pieces finally came together.

The image of Charlie's pinched little face came back to her, hurt and determined to clear her brother. Brave little girl, unwavering in her faith in Ricky.

She glanced up to find the same clear gray eyes as Charlie's looking at her. Ricky shrugged. "With all due respect, I didn't expect you to come up with anything. A bit too much to hope for."

"Don't give up on me yet," Georgie said. "We psychic detectives have flashes of brilliance, you know."

"Help from beyond," he said whimsically. Then a thought seemed to occur to him, and his eyes narrowed slightly. "Psychic detective. I wonder if I could base a new character on that?"

Georgie laughed. "Don't you start. It's enough to have Jaxx Saxby trying to talk me into being part of her new series. Now you want to turn me into a character for a computer game?"

"Everyone and everything I meet is fodder," he said, "including bad guys planting drugs." He gestured at his computer. "Would you like to see what I do?"

"I'd love to." She beamed at him. "Show me how you can buy and sell real estate and characters that don't exist. Who would have thought?"

And while she was being introduced to Ricky's virtual world, she thought, she would keep her senses alert for any clues about why his real world was falling to pieces.

CHAPTER 9

The Draper Twins

Back at the Draper vintage open day, Tammy's mind was going at a million miles a minute while she figured out the best way to handle Jonathan's mother. Whichever way she looked at it, the outcome was doomed. A photographer had just captured the rich and elegant Madelyn Draper in her fabulous expensive vintage 20s dress, glaring at Rockabilly Princess Tammy Dyson in a knockoff of the same dress, perched next to Madelyn's favorite son in Madelyn's husband's favorite car.

They even had almost-the-same blonde hair set in 20s finger waves.

Get me out of here, thought Tammy, but said, "Mrs. Draper! You look wonderful. I see we have similar taste." She cringed at the quick flash of animosity in Madelyn's eyes. *Oops. Wrong thing to say.*

Madelyn tilted her chin and raised a haughty eyebrow while smiling sweetly. "It is a beautiful dress, yes, but I thought I had the only original."

"I'm sure you do," agreed Tammy, thinking fast. "I fell in love with it when I saw it on the Internet, so I ran up a copy on my sewing machine. Of course, the finish wouldn't be anything like yours."

"You saw it on the Internet?" Madelyn's smile became fixed. "On my Facebook page, perhaps?"

Worse and worse.

"No, actually," Tammy said. "On a Pinterest Vintage Fashion board." Desperate to escape and conscious of the photographer still hovering in the background, she turned to Jonathan, who was watching the exchange. "Jonathan, if I can manage to extract myself from this gorgeous car, I'd love to see the vintage trailers."

"Excellent idea," he agreed, a little too heartily. "I know Charlotte has been dying to show them to you, so I'll round her up." He turned his Ken doll smile up to 'supercharged' and grinned at his mother. "Mom and Dad and I get photos taken every year with various cars in the collection, so we'll be busy for a while. I'll catch up with you later."

She had to admire his skill in rescuing the moment. Within minutes he had her out of the car and had located Charlie—who was all too delighted to be rescued from wandering around with trays of canapés—and dispatched them to the vintage trailer bays. A backward glance showed Madelyn preening and laughing with Jonathan's arm around her shoulder.

Charlie saw her looking.

"You and Mom are wearing the same dress," she observed. "She won't like that. She bought it especially for today."

"I wouldn't have worn it if I'd known," Tammy said helplessly.

"She'll get over it." Charlie's voice was indifferent. No doubt she'd had years of having to wait for her mother to get over various imagined slights. She glanced down at her own outfit, a fringed sheath reminiscent of the Flapper era. "Serves her right for making me wear this. Beth and I always have to dress to match Mom's outfit. I wanted to wear boy's clothes, but she wouldn't let me. I hate dresses."

They rounded the corner, and Tammy forgot Madelyn the moment she saw the vintage trailers. They were just as immaculate as the Draper classic cars, ranging from a gleaming Westcraft Trolley Top to a cute teardrop style. Charlie displayed an incredible amount of knowledge for a girl just shy of her thirteenth birthday. She chattered away as they stepped in and out of the trailers, just as confident with her discussion of sourcing authentic parts and rebuilding rotting frames as any veteran.

"That's it for Dad's trailers," Charlie said as they left the last one. "Now, you want to see *mine*?" Her grin was as wide as the sky.

"What, there's more?" Tammy feigned amazement, enjoying Charlie's excitement. "I think I've died and gone to heaven. Show me!"

"This way." Charlie sped off around a corner of the house and through a gate that led to a lawn big enough to serve as a golf course. In the far corner, bordered by a low brick wall, Tammy could see a flash of color amongst some flowering shrubs.

As she got closer, one of the most darling trailers she had ever seen was revealed, painted in golden yellow and white with a gaily-striped awning in the same colors. Underneath the awning was a mat with bright scatter cushions in blue and gold, and director's chairs upholstered in the same striped fabric as the awning, grouped around a small square white table. On the table was a platter of mixed sandwiches and finger food and a bottle of soda. All around the trailer, bright flowers spilled out of yellow and blue pots.

Heaven.

"It's a 1955 Bellwood travel trailer," Charlie told

her with pride. "I loved it so much Dad said he'd give it to us."

"Surprise!" Laughing, Beth Draper appeared in the doorway, flinging up one arm and pouting in a perfect 20s Flapper pose before she jumped down to meet them. Grinning at her twin, she said with satisfaction, "I knew you'd bring Tammy here!"

Young Elizabeth Draper was dressed in the same outfit as Charlie but looked much more at home in hers, with her shining gold hair held back with a headband decorated with a flower made of pearls. She jerked a thumb back toward the trailer. "I sneaked us some food and drinks so that we can have a picnic!"

"Like we'll get away with that on Mom's vintage open day," Charlie said skeptically. "How long do you reckon we've got until she drags us back?"

"Oh, you." Unfazed by Charlie's lukewarm reception, Beth punched her lightly on the arm. "We'd better be quick, then. I'll get some glasses. Come and see inside, Tammy! Charlie worked on this for *ages!* I helped choose the colors. Do you like them?"

Tammy followed Beth, with Charlie hot on her heels, enjoying the twins' enthusiasm. Charlie gave a running commentary on the history of the trailer, the restoration process, and how they'd made their

Dad give in on the colors: "He wanted authentic colors, but we wanted yellow!".

At the same time, Beth bounced around demonstrating the beds' comfort and took selfies with her phone. "Only eleven more days, and we can have a Facebook page!" she announced. "I can't wait!"

"I can," muttered Charlie dourly.

"But just think, Charlie, you can put up pictures of all your trailers!" Beth rolled her eyes comically. "Sandpaper and glue and hammers and stuff. Working with Dad."

"And you can fill it with selfies in a thousand different outfits," returned Charlie, before both girls broke out into identical giggles.

They were a fantastic couple of kids, thought Tammy warmly. Whatever their mother was like, these two were happy to be themselves.

As it turned out, Charlie was right; their escape didn't last long. A scant fifteen minutes after they got there, Madelyn sent her stormtroopers to extract the girls and return them to their hostessing duties.

"Uh oh," Charlie said, looking past Tammy's shoulder. "Here comes Tyler." Her eyebrows drew together, and her forehead lowered.

"And Alexis," contributed Beth. "They have

that serious look. We're in trouble." She warbled the last word, not sounding at all concerned.

Tammy turned and watched the two hiking across the lawn; a girl in her early twenties in a suit featuring the big shoulder pads of the forties and a man who was clearly her brother, clad in a striped suit and fedora. "Who are Tyler and Alexis?"

"Our cousins," the twins said together.

On Madelyn's side, Tammy guessed, seeing the faint resemblance to Jonathan. The two were like faded photocopies of the gorgeous half of the Draper family.

When the two reached them, Alexis spoke directly to the girls, ignoring Tammy. "Your mother wants you two back at the house right now."

"Hi," Tammy said, instinctively disliking her. "I'm Tammy."

Alexis gave a short nod, dismissing her with a glance.

"And you are…?" enquired Tammy. If there was one thing that made her hackles rise, it was rudeness.

"Alexis," the girl bit out, her hazel eyes cold. "Charlotte, you've spilled something on your dress. Look at that." She stabbed a finger at a mayonnaise stain staining the silk right in the center of Charlie's chest.

"Don't I always?" Charlie stared back challengingly.

"You're hopeless." Alexis turned her attention to Beth, her voice warming slightly. "Come on, Elizabeth, you know you shouldn't be here. You have a job to do."

Tyler had been standing back a little, saying nothing, but Tammy could feel his stare drilling into her. He moved forward, and as his eyes met hers, she felt a cold shiver go down her back. There was a coldness in his gaze that made her blood freeze and caused her breath to catch in her throat.

She had known only one other person in her life with that kind of darkness in his soul, and she had spent the past ten years trying to get past it.

He moved forward and extended his hand. "Hello. Tammy, is it? I'm Tyler."

Reluctantly, she shook his hand once and pulled back. It was like touching the dry, smooth skin of a snake. She gave him a lukewarm smile and said nothing.

His lip curled in a facsimile of a smile, knowing exactly the effect he was having on her. "Where are you from, Tammy?"

"Louisiana," she said shortly.

"Louisiana." He rolled the word around on his tongue, making it sound as though she'd said,

'Folsom Prison.' "Is your family interested in classic cars too?"

"No."

He opened his mouth to ask more questions but was forestalled by an exclamation from Beth. "Oh, goodie, here comes the photographer. He can get some pictures of us all together here with our trailer." She poked Charlie, obviously anticipating her objection. "Facebook, Charlie. You want a picture of Tammy on it, don't you?"

Alexis snorted. "Charlie never wants a photo of herself anywhere." Her expression said, *and with good reason.*

Tammy wanted to kick her. Instead, she turned to Charlie. "Charlie, would you mind? I'd love a photo. I have a feeling you're going to be one of the go-to people for vintage trailer restorations in the future." She winked. "I want to be able to say I knew you when you were just starting!"

Charlie's rebellious expression softened, and a faint blush of pleasure stained her cheeks. "I'm not that good."

"Yes, you are," Tammy said firmly. If she could just get Charlie to give that huge, transformational smile for the camera, it would make all the difference. "Come on. Let's go pose near the trailer." With a friendly nudge, she added in a stage whisper,

"I want this for my own Facebook page!" She shot a look at Alexis, not being able to bring herself to look at Tyler. "Alexis, if you and Tyler wouldn't mind giving us just a few more minutes…? We won't be long."

Charlie, intelligent enough to understand the undercurrents, was instantly motivated to join in the conspiracy. Clearly, she wasn't fond of her cousins. "OK. Just one."

The photographer, who looked thrilled that they were making his life so easy, clicked off half a dozen shots before they all obeyed Madelyn's edict and went back to the party.

If Tammy had known the consequences of those innocent photos, she would have tackled him, ripped the card out of his camera, and swallowed it.

CHAPTER 10

A Hanging Offense

Somehow Tammy got through the next few hours, smiling for the cameras, lunching with Jonathan at her elbow, and spending a tolerable half-hour with Douglas Draper and his cronies. The whole time she was conscious of assorted cold looks from Madelyn, Alexis, and Tyler.

She could have simply made her excuses and left, but Tammy Dyson was made of sterner stuff. It wasn't her way to give in to bullies and snobs—but she was limp with relief when she finally waved a cheerful goodbye to Jonathan, flanked by the twins, and drove away.

"OMG," she said to her reflection in the rearview mirror, widening her eyes. "What an ordeal!"

No matter how gorgeous and entertaining

Jonathan Draper was, his mother simply wasn't worth it. Talk about the mother-in-law from hell. She felt sorry for the poor girl who *did* end up Jonathan's wife. She'd better be loaded and influential. However, that might make Madelyn even more spiteful.

She blew out a deep breath and punched up some Jerry Lee Lewis. Fifties rock, that's what she needed. For the first time in living memory, she couldn't wait to swap her vintage clothes for something ordinary—anything but the white 20s sheath she wore.

Imagine having the impossibly lousy luck to turn up in a cheap duplicate of Madelyn Draper's vintage dress.

Agh.

She banged her head back against the headrest a couple of times, turned up the volume, and joined in the chorus. "*Goodness, gracious, great balls of fire!*"

She couldn't have phrased it better herself.

When she got back to the RV park, the retro social life was in full swing. Georgie and Layla were flat out with prospective buyers and immediately waved her over to chat about colors and soft furnishings.

Goodbye to the rest of the day, Tammy thought and dived in to help.

Sales talk and orders gave way to Happy Hour, which morphed into a cookout for supper, and by the time they finally met up in Tammy's trailer that night, it was almost nine-thirty.

Layla kicked off her shoes and headed straight for the bed, throwing herself back on the pillows with a groan. "What a day! I'm dead. Car trouble for two days, in hock on my credit card to fix it, up at dawn this morning to hook up, drive drive drive, get here to be attacked by rabid vintage wannabes —remind me why I wanted this job, again?"

Trixxi struggled out of Tammy's arms, bounded up towards Layla, and scrabbled at the side of the bed with a few plaintive whines.

Layla opened an eye. "What's the matter, short stuff? Can't quite make it up here with the big girls?" She rolled over, scooped up the toy poodle, and rolled back, setting Trixxi on her chest and stroking her. "Love your Auntie Layla, don't you?" She closed her eyes and sighed.

"Don't go to sleep," Tammy said unfeelingly. "We have work to do."

"Been working," Layla mumbled. "Tired. Sleep time."

"You can sleep when you're dead," said Georgie

and Tammy in unison. "That's the new motto for the Crystal Ball Investigation Team," Georgie added.

"OK, OK. I'm listening. Fill me in." Layla didn't open her eyes.

"Let's keep it short," suggested Georgie, "seeing as how we're all tired, and we'll have to go over it all with Scott tomorrow anyway. I'll go first."

She ran through her visit with the infamous Ricky Draper, official Black Sheep of the Draper household. Tammy fixed her eyes on Georgie's face, reading her expression, until she finished. Layla opened one eye, then two, and finally grew interested enough to wriggle into a sitting position, punching up the pillows behind her. "Someone framed him for a drug bust?" she said. "What an awful thing to do. As if the jewelry wasn't bad enough."

Tammy cut straight to the chase. "You say he suspects Jonathan?"

"Not exactly," Georgie clarified. "He said he *would* have suspected Jonathan, but he was with the rest of the family on the other side of the country."

"But when you were doing a reading, you got a bad feeling about his cousins? Tyler and Alexis?"

"Definitely," Georgie said. "It was instant. Just a

"these two are bad news" feeling." She narrowed her eyes at Tammy. "OK, I can tell you're bursting. Give it up."

Tammy sighed. Sharing her day with her two best friends could only help.

"I think you're right about the cousins," she started. "But let me tell you how *my* day played out. First, Madelyn Draper is a snake. Second, the niece and nephew Alexis and Tyler are following in her footsteps. Third, Jonathan is a question mark." She looked at Georgie. "You know how Jerry always drove you nuts as a kid? Put the blame on you, led you into mischief, set you up, cheated at games—all that kind of thing?"

Georgie grinned back at her, momentarily diverted. "And yet you want to marry him."

"No," Tammy said, "*he* wants to marry me. But that's beside the point. Anyway, that's your brother Jerry, right? Or was. I do think he might have improved."

"Sounds about right," Georgie conceded. "He was far from the perfect big brother."

"Well, that's the feeling I'm getting about Jonathan, only maybe a bit worse. He'll twist things to get his way, and he'll manipulate people, but set Ricky up to go to prison?" She shrugged. "I can't see it. But..." she swallowed, remembering the flat look in Tyler's eyes. "I can see Tyler doing it. And Alexis would probably tag along with him."

Georgie mimed writing on a whiteboard. "Chief suspects: Tyler and Alexis. We need to check whether they were around at the time of the jewelry theft, but even if they were, apparently Ricky was the only one who showed up on the security video. And when you talk to him, he comes up against the same roadblock as I do: the *why*. If it *was* Tyler and Alexis -*why*?

"Evil for evil's sake?" Tammy shrugged. "But they seem to be pretty thick with the Draper family. Or Madelyn, anyway. Let's dig a bit and see what we can find out about them. The whole family. There's *got* to be a reason."

"OK." Georgie looked thoughtful. "And we need to chase up the man with the black cat. Why did he appear in the crystal ball?"

"A man with a black cat." Layla scratched Trixxi behind the ears, getting a blissed-out groan in response. "That's like saying, "Look for a woman with a white dog."

"It could be one of those narrowing-down things." Georgie drew a circle around the words' man with black cat' on her notebook. "It might be relevant later."

Her words were interrupted by a few musical

chimes from Tammy's phone. She picked it up, swiped and found herself looking at Jerry's face. "It's Jerry." She flicked it on and said, still a little coolly because he was with Jaxx Saxby, "Hi, Jerry." However, the greeting wasn't quite as cool as it would have been before she met Madelyn Draper and her niece and nephew. Jerry shone in comparison.

"What the hell have you been up to now?" came Jerry's annoyed voice, loud enough for them all to hear. "For God's sake, Tammy. Jonathan *Draper?*"

"And hello to you too," said Tammy crossly, hit the red button, and tossed the phone aside. After the kind of day she'd had, she wasn't going to have a conversation with anyone who began with, *'What the hell have you been up to?'"*

Georgie nodded approvingly. "Good move."

"You see what it'd be like if I married him?" Tammy opened her hands in frustration. "One minute he's a prince, the next minute he's yelling at me." She frowned at Georgie. "Scott doesn't do that to you."

"No, but Scott is probably the most laid-back person on the face of the planet," Georgie pointed out. "Jerry's Jerry."

"Although," Layla mused from the bed, amusing

herself by re-tying the red polka-dot ribbon on Trixxi's topknot, "he has improved. I remember the first time I met him; he was trying to steal your customers, Georgie."

"Well, that hasn't changed," she said with a wry smile. "It's a game to Jerry. If he could make off with a commission under my nose, he would. Just for the sport. Although I'm not sure if he'd dare do it to Tammy."

"Yeah, he would," said Tammy with feeling. "Plenty of games and one-upmanship in our household. Which is mostly fun, but Jerry still kind of doesn't know where to draw the line."

Her phone rang again.

They all stared at it. Tammy waited for three more rings, picked it up, and then tapped the green button under Jerry's face. "Hello, Tammy Dyson speaking."

"Dammit, Tammy, you know it's me! And don't hang up. I've sent you a link by email. Check it out and get back to me." He severed the connection.

Surprised, she looked at the phone. "He hung up."

"Must be serious," Layla said. "Check it."

Tammy switched apps and read Jerry's email. "Someone tagged him on a Facebook page post." She tapped the link.

She was looking at the Facebook page belonging to the photographer that had been chasing her around at the Draper open day. Ossie McManus… the name sounded vaguely familiar. Her heart sinking, she scrolled down the page.

Oh, for heaven's sake. The man had a social gossip page. He wasn't just a photographer; he was a leading pot-stirrer. But this time, he'd excelled.

"Oh, *man.*" She skimmed through three or four posts about the Draper bash.

Tammy was lifted into the classic Raceabout by a grinning Jonathan Draper, showing a lot more leg than she would have wished. And there was Madelyn, her face grim with fury as she stared at Tammy. Under the photo was the caption: "Young, beautiful, and wearing the same dress as the hostess—a hanging offense?"

There was lots more about Jonathan Draper's status as an eligible bachelor, surmise about Tammy's relationship with Jerry B. Goode, and to cap it all off, a photo of Tammy with an arm around each of the Draper twins in front of their vintage trailer playhouse. It was a nice photo. Beth looked gorgeous, and Charlie's wide smile gave her face character.

The accompanying text was far from pleasant. "Cheerful Charlotte! Usually, Charlotte Draper is the forgotten twin. Today, with her heroine Tammy Dyson of the Johnny B. Goode Vintage Trailer Division admiring her handiwork, Charlie looked uncharacteristically cheerful. Could she be looking forward to having a charming and talented sister-in-law?"

"Oh, for heaven's sake," Tammy said, sliding the phone across to Georgie with a groan. "Kill me now. If you don't, Madelyn Draper will."

Georgie scrolled down the page. "Nice legs, Tams. No wonder Jerry was on the phone in a lather."

"I wanted him to see photos of me with Jonathan," Tammy said. "I didn't want this idiot to start talking about me being the girls' *sister-in-law.*" She buried her head in her hands. "I hate social media!"

Georgie tossed the phone across to Layla. "Look on the bright side, Tams. You start stirring the pot; you never know what might bubble to the top."

CHAPTER 11

The Gossip Mill

When the others left, Tammy didn't go to bed. Her blood was up.

How dare this social media slimeball do this to her? And she'd been so *nice* to him, thinking he was the official photographer.

Although technically, he hadn't done it to her; he'd done it to Madelyn—and it was probably well and truly her turn to find herself at the end of his acid observations. When Tammy spent some time on his Facebook page, she discovered that many of his posts had made Madelyn look good at the expense of others who graced the social scene. He *had* had a subtle dig at her a few times, but she had the feeling it was just to maintain the appearance of being impartial.

Scroll, scroll, click, click.

What she couldn't figure out was why anyone would invite someone like him to *any* social do. The Draper open day had been invitation-only; it wasn't as though he could just gatecrash.

"Play with fire, and you get burned, Madelyn," she murmured.

Trixxi, on the seat beside her, raised her head for a second, then thumped it down on her paws with a heavy sigh. Tammy reached over and absently rubbed the dog's head while following the trail of someone who did a lot of commenting about Madelyn. "There are quite a few people who don't like Madelyn Draper, Trixxi; imagine that."

Click, click, click.

When she finished, she had a list of half a dozen names to contact, particularly those that had commented more than a few times about the Draper children. *Someone* would know the gossip.

Her phone buzzed.

Tammy flicked to messages. Jerry again.

Flying out tomorrow, he had texted. *Wait for me.*

She gritted her teeth. The last thing she needed was Jerry arriving to grill her about what she'd been doing with Jonathan Draper. Had *she* been on his back about his so-called shakedown trip with Jaxx Saxby and her botoxed lips and her cursed Dancing With the Stars trophy? No.

Had he shown the tiniest glimmer of insight into her feelings about watching him chase Jaxx and her mammoth motorhome around the country? *No.*

She was about to send a text saying *Won't be here* when the phone buzzed again in her hand, and another message popped up—just one word.

Please.

Tammy stared at it.

Funny, the difference one word could make.

Her fingers hovered over the screen while she thought about Jonathan and Madelyn and especially about creepy Tyler.

She texted back *OK.*

The following day the three of them got together for a quick meeting in Georgie's gypsy trailer, shutting the door against the happy buzz of the retro crowd setting up for a communal breakfast in the camp kitchen.

"We're expected to join them out there," Georgie said, "so we only have time for a quick meeting to decide what we're going to do. One of us will have to draw the raffle prize after breakfast, too." She looked at Tammy. "What is it, by the way?"

"Consultation with our restoration team and two thousand dollars worth of work," Tammy said, "or the same value in fittings if they want to do the work themselves."

"We'll have to stick around most of the day. I have a few more people to catch up with," Layla said. "No formal appointments. I've just said, 'grab me when you see me around,' so I need to be here."

"Same here," Georgie said. "Which won't leave us much time to keep following up Ricky's case. But I was thinking, why not turn it to our advantage? This place is full of people who know the Drapers, and a lot of them were at their open day yesterday. Let's see what we can find out before Scott gets here."

"And Jerry," Tammy put in.

Georgie stared at her. Tammy's face was giving nothing away. "Jerry's coming here?"

"He's flying out. He'll be here late afternoon." She shrugged. "It might defuse some of the gossip."

"Or add fuel to it," Georgie pointed out. "What happened to Jaxx?"

"No idea. Well, she's had him for a week; how long can she expect a manufacturer to follow her around in case something goes wrong?" Tammy flapped a hand. "Silly question, we're talking about

Jaxx Saxby. The answer is 'as long as she wants' when she's paying over a million for the wheels. Or her daddy is, anyway."

"You know," Georgie said thoughtfully, "having Jerry here could be a plus. We'll tell him what's going on, and he can mingle with the crowd and play the wronged boyfriend slash eligible bachelor." She looked around. "Any new thoughts about yesterday's events?"

Tammy handed over her list of names. "These are people who had a go at Madelyn on that Facebook page. I followed up dozens of names, but these kept coming up. I thought I'd try to contact them."

Georgie scanned the list and pointed at one of them. "You lucked in. Cassie Rhineberger is here, the pint-sized redhead in the vintage Airstream over near the gate." Her finger moved down. "So is Jan Keeley. 1950s Shasta. Great laugh, over-the-top personality. You'll hear her before you see her."

"Perfect," Tammy said. "I'll see if I can sit near one of them at breakfast."

As it turned out, Tammy didn't have to look for Jan Keeley. The other woman took the first opportunity to pounce on *her*.

"Tammy Dyson!" a voice boomed in her ear as Tammy waited in the queue, chatting and laughing with others around her.

Tammy turned with a smile. "Yes?"

"Perhaps I should say 'the infamous Tammy Dyson', said the woman, beaming at her. Her blonde hair was tucked up into a turquoise bandana, and she had squeezed her ample figure into tight black pedal pushers and a fitted turquoise shirt with a black collar. "You sure got up Madelyn's nose yesterday."

"Keep it down, Jan," said the woman in front of Tammy, glancing around her. "The Drapers are here, you know."

Jan Keeley snorted. "No, they're not. Their trailer's still here, but they're at their house."

"Even so, they have friends here," the other woman pointed out in a low voice. "You want to start a fight with Madelyn? I sure wouldn't."

This was getting interesting already, Tammy thought. She smiled at Jan. "It was all a storm in a teacup. You know how social media gets out of hand."

"I know how Ossie *McManus* can get out of

hand," Jan said, sparks flashing in her eyes. "Man's a menace. Are you honestly taking up with Jonathan? What happened to Jerry Goode?"

The woman who had told Jan to keep it down rolled her eyes. *"Jan."*

"I'm only asking what everyone else wants to know," Jan said, unrepentant. She seized Tammy by the arm. "You booked up for breakfast?"

"Um, no." It was all Tammy could do not to laugh out loud. Jan Keeley had a big personality, all right. "What about you?"

"Am now," Jan said with a wink. She pointed at the end of a long table. "Over there. That's my pink bag."

"Great," Tammy said. "You can tell me all about Ossie McManus." *And,* she thought, *the Draper family.*

"Quid pro quo," Jan chirped. "I want the dirt on Jerry Goode."

This time Tammy did laugh. "Done."

The two of them collected their cooked breakfast from the efficient crew operating the grills and headed for Jan's pink bag.

When Georgie saw Tammy being borne off by Jan Keeley, she decided to target the other name on Tammy's list: Cassie Rhineberger. She might as well start with the ones who had fired salvos on social media.

Cassie, however, proved somewhat elusive. She wasn't in the breakfast queue, and she wasn't anywhere near her Airstream. She didn't appear to be anywhere in the RV park.

Georgie's progress was slow since she was hailed by the many people who knew her from the RV Empire ads and retro scene. A few asked if she was still telling fortunes. Her diplomatic answer to that was, "Sometimes, but I'm a bit busy this weekend." Layla, seeing her predicament, caught up with her long enough to shove a plate of food into her hand and point her at a seat. She had just cleared her plate and answered a dozen questions about their vintage trailer models when she spotted Cassie pulling up near her Airstream and getting out of the car with a couple of shopping bags. She waved at one of the organizers, pointed to the bags, and gave a thumbs-up before heading for the fridge in the camp kitchen, not far from where Georgie was sitting.

Mystery solved, Georgie thought, watching her

unpack milk and bread. She'd just nipped out for extra supplies.

"Georgie?" Lori, the secretary of the organizing committee, tapped her on the shoulder. "Would you like to draw the raffle now before half of them disappear to do some sightseeing?"

"Sure." Perfect timing, Georgie thought, seeing Cassie heading her way. She jumped up and put out a hand to forestall Cassie, who was busy tying on an apron with a heart-shaped bib and a gingham frill.

"Excuse me…?"

She stopped, one eyebrow raised.

"Lori has just asked me to draw the raffle," Georgie said swiftly. "I'd love it if one of the worker bees here could pull out the winning ticket. Would you mind?"

"Why, sure! Love to." Cassie grinned. "Hope it's mine. I've got a brand new project starting soon."

She walked across to the mic with Georgie.

The crowd hushed expectantly and watched while Georgie grabbed a white-painted wicker basket lined with red polka dot cotton, filled with raffle tickets. "Ready, Cassie? Here we go!" She raised it above eye-level.

Cassie played the crowd, blowing on her fingers and flexing them a few times, showing the group she had nothing in her hands ("no tickets up my sleeve!") before plunging her hand in and pulling out a pale pink ticket.

She put her hand to her mouth and clutched the hand with the ticket to her chest. "Oh, *please*…mine was pink! Could I be that lucky?"

Amidst good-natured laughter, she opened up the ticket.

"Well, Cassie?" Georgie said in amusement. "Is it yours?"

Cassie bit her lip. She shook her head, sighed, and handed the ticket to Georgie. "'Fraid not." She mimed colossal disappointment.

Georgie patted her sympathetically and read out the name on the ticket. "The winner: Lisa Andretti!"

There was a wild cheer from a table in the midst of the group, and a dark-haired woman rocketed up out of her seat, punching the air. "I won! I won!" She hurried up to claim the envelope with the prize voucher, with much high-fiving on the way.

As the crowd began to disperse, Georgie turned to Cassie. "I'd love to see what you've done with your Airstream. I'm sure Tammy would too. And maybe we can toss around a few ideas for your next project?"

Cassie glanced over to where Tammy was still

listening to a long and loud discourse by Jan Keeley, her smile looking somewhat fixed. The grin on Cassie's freckled face faded, and the good-humored expression in her eyes gave way to something more serious. "You know, I was already planning to catch up with Tammy today if I could. Let me help the girls finish up here in the kitchen, and I'll show you both through the Airstream. Say half an hour?"

"Done," Georgie said. "See you there."

Watching Cassie walk away, she didn't need her crystal ball to know that the meeting would be about more than fitting out vintage trailers.

CHAPTER 12

A Glimpse into the Past

Cassie ushered them both inside her trailer and firmly closed the door behind them. Georgie and Tammy shot a quick look at each other: at a rally, people never did this unless they wanted privacy. Usually, they were only too keen to show off their vintage treasures to anyone walking by.

And Cassie Rhineberger's trailer *was* a treasure. The interior was immaculate, from the upholstery on the seats to the curtain fabric, the colors faithfully replicating those from the day it was built. Everything, from the Bopp Decker Vacron pitcher and glasses to the art deco radio, reflected the era— including Cassie's flower-sprigged dress with the nipped-in waist and full skirt and her ginger curls caught up with a floral clasp.

"Wow, Cassie," Tammy said, her eyes shining. "This is perfect. I don't think you need our advice. We should recruit you for the team instead!" She picked up one of the glasses arranged on a tray, turning it around carefully in her hands to inspect it. "I've been haunting eBay for a set of these."

"I was on the hunt for them for ages before I found them, too." Cassie beamed, looking proudly around her trailer. "I love them. But Ray has just bought a Mustang to restore, and that means I'll have a whole new project too. We're looking for a trailer to go with it now so that we can do matching colors."

They took a few more minutes to inspect the trailer and then sat at the table to look through Cassie's photos of the restoration process, but Georgie was conscious of the growing tension on the other woman's face.

Finally, Cassie closed the album and got to the point. "I hope you don't mind, Tammy, but I wanted to alert you to something that came up on Facebook yesterday."

Tammy rolled her eyes. "The Ossie McManus column."

"Oh, you've seen it then?" Cassie's eyes searched Tammy's face, looking for a reaction.

"Jerry sent me a text last night."

"Oh." There was a world of understanding in that one short word.

"I spent some time reading through the column after that," Tammy told her and then took the bull by the horns. "I notice that you've responded with a few comments from time to time when Madelyn Draper's name appears."

"I try not to engage, most of the time." Cassie tucked a few errant curls behind her ear, her eyes cool. "But sometimes I can't help myself. She gets away with far too much, and Ossie's well and truly in her pocket. I was surprised that he made that crack about you both wearing the same dress. She'll make him pay for that." A grim smile crossed her face. "Maybe her pet columnist is getting sick of her."

"How long have you known her?" asked Georgie curiously.

Cassie shrugged. "Forever. My husband Ray and Douglas Draper are crazy about classic cars – except Ray spends only a fraction of what Douglas does. They're good friends, which makes it awkward. Sometimes we have no choice but to be at the same event. Like this one." She shot a look at Tammy. "I just wanted to warn you: don't take her lightly. If she takes a dislike to you, she'll keep after you. She's ruined others."

Georgie thought of Charlie's earnest face as she had begged Georgie to help her brother and said, "Do you know much about Madelyn's kids, Cassie?"

"I know a *lot* about her kids," Cassie said, folding her arms. "My Alex was Ricky Draper's best friend all through elementary school—high school as well, until Ricky went off the rails. How much do you want to know?"

Next to Georgie, Tammy sat forward, reflecting Georgie's excitement. This was it; they could both feel it. The breakthrough they needed

"That's a good place to start," Georgie said. "Ricky Draper. We know he's estranged from the family. Were you surprised when he started keeping company with the wrong crowd?"

Cassie took a moment before replying, studying Georgie's face. "This is about more than last night's Facebook post, isn't it?"

Georgie did her the courtesy of being honest. "Yes. Thanks to his sister, we've met Ricky, and we're trying to help him. He's been in a spot of trouble, but Charlie doesn't believe he did what they say he did. And for what it's worth, neither do I."

Cassie closed her eyes and blew out a long breath. "At last, that poor boy might get some justice. Good on Charlie. She's a gorgeous kid. Madelyn hates her, of course."

Startled, Georgie exchanged a look with Tammy. "She *hates* her?"

"I honestly don't think that's too strong a judgment," Cassie said sadly. "With Madelyn, everything has to be perfect. Including her children. Charlie is a plain child, but she was an even plainer baby. Her mother virtually ignored her."

"Horrible woman. Some people should be drowned at birth," said Tammy heatedly.

"She was the same with Ricky; I've known her since our two boys were tiny. She never picked him up unless she had to, never engaged with him. Then just over a year later, Jonathan came along, and it was as though she had only one child. It was the same with the twins: Elizabeth got all the attention. Only her "perfect" children were worth spending time with." There was a glint of tears in her eyes. "I lost my temper one day when the girls were tiny and said something to her. From that day on, she wouldn't let Ricky come over to hang out with Alex. Their friendship stalled, and it wasn't long after that Ricky started to act out."

"But what about Douglas?" asked Tammy. "He must have noticed what was going on."

"He worked long hours building up his

gaming business, and she was always careful when he was around. I'm sure she's more careful with Charlie now because Douglas dotes on her." Cassie gave a short laugh. "Douglas gives Madelyn everything she wants; she's not going to risk her meal ticket. She wants the best and gets the best."

Georgie mulled over what she'd just heard, wondering how much Cassie knew. "Cassie, do you know *why* Ricky has been virtually excommunicated?"

"The jewelry thing? Madelyn made sure it got out, although she pretended they were trying to hush it up. She'll do anything to discredit Ricky. She wants him out permanently."

Georgie asked the question burning in her mind —the question that she was beginning to feel she already knew the answer to. "So, who do you think took the jewelry?"

Cassie didn't even hesitate. "Look at Madelyn or that nasty nephew of hers. I have no idea how they set it up, but one of them will be behind it. I just wish I could prove it."

As she said the words, Georgie had a quick mental image of her crystal ball, resting quietly in the shadows 0n its shelf in her gypsy trailer.

It was almost as though it was calling to her.

Now that she was on the right track, maybe it was time for another reading.

Bands of color from the stained glass windows slanted across the table and made the crystal ball glow in shades of green and blue. For a moment, Georgie felt that she was looking into the depths of a deep, serene lake.

Gently, she trailed her fingertips across the hard glass surface and caught her breath when she felt a sensation of warmth. There *was* something ready to come through.

Not pictures, this time. But perhaps she didn't need pictures; she could clearly remember what had come through last time: the image of the vintage Rolls, with the Draper family gathered around it.

Now, though, she knew the truth behind that family scene. Ricky and Charlie on one side, Jonathan and Elizabeth on the other. The way it had always been in the Draper household: Madelyn's 'perfect' children set apart from the not-so-perfect.

Cassie's words came back to her: *She hates Charlie.*

How could anyone hate that talented, wonderful child?

Georgie let herself drift. She needed something to show her how to restore Ricky's good name.

And preferably, to expose Madelyn for what she was.

Suddenly, a voice she knew all too well sounded in her mind. *Ask Jerry.*

Georgie's eyes flew open. *Rosa?* When she had first started using her hand-me-down crystal ball, she had become accustomed to hearing her great-grandmother's voice echoing in her mind. It had almost seemed that Rosa was guiding her. But the last time had been months and months ago. Nearly a year, she realized.

Ask your brother, came the voice again, now fading. *Remember the cat.*

Remember the cat? She and Jerry had never owned a cat. It had always been dogs in their household.

Drift, Georgie, drift. She knew better than to try to force it; that could bring only disappointment.

Cat.

The man with the black cat, in her last reading! *That* must be the cat.

Maybe Jerry knew someone with a black cat?

Two images in quick succession blinked through

her mind: the man with the cat and the two pale blonde Draper cousins.

She stared at the crystal ball, still gleaming in reflected shades of blue and green—no mist inside it, no pictures to help her.

Ask Jerry.

"All right, Rosa," she said aloud. "Jerry, it will be."

CHAPTER 13

The Man with the Cat

Scott and Jerry both arrived about the same time, but nobody had a chance to talk to Jerry before the retro crowd swamped him. More than a few of them had read the posts on Ossie's Facebook post and cast speculative glances at him and Tammy.

Jerry guessed what they were thinking and promptly defused speculation by staying close to Tammy's side. Georgie heard him hiss into her ear, "Play up to me, Tams," and was tempted to pat him on the back. Sure, she could have strung him up when he went haring off after Jaxx Saxby, but that *had* been work.

She supposed.

When she finally made her way to Scott's

camper, she blinked at the sight of his face. "Wow, that's some black eye. Does it hurt?"

He shrugged. "A bit. It's OK." He gave her a hug and a kiss. "How are things going? No bad guys chasing you, I hope?"

"Not me; they're after Tammy." She looked at him searchingly, knowing he'd been driving long hours. "Tired?"

"Good to be able to stop." He gave a dismissive wave. "Tell me what's going on."

She found a quiet corner and filled him in, including the final cryptic message from Rosa. "So we have to ask Jerry about a man with a cat. God knows why."

Scott smiled and tapped her on the nose. "Jerry's been around. He probably knows lots of guys with cats."

Finally, she caught a signal from Tammy and gave her a wave.

"We're on," she said. "We're meeting in Tammy's trailer. It has the most room since Jerry doesn't have his motorhome with him. Let's see what we can find out."

Away from the crowds, Tammy and Jerry kept their distance from each other. Georgie watched them covertly. Tammy was still miffed. Jerry had his poker face on, which usually meant that he was annoyed.

All right then, she would start. Give Tammy some breathing room.

"OK," she said. "I've filled Scott in, and Tammy's briefed Layla, but let's run through the whole thing. Feel free to butt in if there's something I miss."

She recapped the initial meeting with Charlie Draper, followed by the chat with Ricky-the-black-sheep. "I'm convinced he's innocent," she said. "I was pretty sure before Tammy and I talked with Cassie Rhineberger today, but now…" she shrugged. "Madelyn seems to be a monster in disguise, although her nephew is more overt about what he does. We have absolutely no proof, though. Tams, can you give your impressions of the Drapers from your day out there?"

Tammy did so, focusing on Madelyn's anger and her treatment by the Draper cousins. She finished with a brief account of her breakfast with Jan Keeley. "She can't stand Madelyn Draper and doesn't care who knows it," she said. "But there was nothing there of value; just a hate-fest. Cassie's information was much more useful."

"It's sad," said Georgie. "Poor Charlie and Ricky." She smiled grimly. "They don't fit the "Charlotte and Richard" mold that Madelyn would like, that's for sure. Anyway, that's where we're at now, apart from a brief message from Rosa to cap things off. A crystal-ball type of message, not a phone call." She recited Rosa's cryptic words, finishing with "*...ask Jerry*".

"That's all she said?" said Layla. "No explanation? No plan of attack?"

"No, typical Rosa. She likes to drop a hint and then let me run with it." She focused on her brother. "Jerry, your turn. What did she mean, ask you? What man with a cat? Can you shed any light on this?"

Jerry looked smug. "I can, as it happens. First, you'd all do well to stay away from the Drapers. Douglas may be harmless, but Madelyn and her sister are pure poison. I've met some nasty people in my time, but they take the cake. Especially Tyler Killock." At Georgie's puzzled look, he clarified, "Madelyn's nephew. Her sister's boy."

Tammy's eyes went dark. "I knew it." She stared down at the table, and they could see her swallow. "He reminds me of my brother."

Jerry looked at her, and his expression softened. Without a word, he reached across and took her hand.

Tammy had never spoken of her family to Georgie, but she had clearly had told Jerry. There was a darkness in Tammy's past. Georgie had resolved never to ask. When Tammy was ready, she'd tell her story. She turned her attention back to Jerry. "How did you meet the Drapers?"

"I went out with Madelyn's sister for a while," he said. "Corinne. She looks very much like Madelyn but with platinum blonde hair. Same as Tyler and Alexis." He thought back. "I would have been around 24, so it was just over ten years ago."

Stunned, Georgie stared at him, crunching numbers. "But Alexis and Tyler are in their twenties...they couldn't have been more than ten or so then. How old is Corinne?"

"She had Tyler at sixteen, Alexis a year later. Think wild child." He shrugged. "That type has a certain appeal. She ran away from home, etcetera —the whole bit. When I met her, she was only in her late twenties. She's a lot younger than Madelyn."

"So you *knew* the Draper kids?"

"I met Jonathan. He and Tyler used to be part-ners in crime. And I do mean partners in crime. I heard things here and there about the two of them. And I've heard more over the years about Tyler." He turned his head to look at Tammy. "That's why I wasn't happy to see Ossie's Facebook posts about you and the Drapers. Tyler and Jonathan are hand-in-glove, and if Tyler isn't in prison by the time he's thirty, it'll be a miracle."

Georgie still couldn't see how they could use what they knew to help Ricky Draper. Even if they suspected Madelyn, how could they prove it? She sat back with a frustrated sigh. "What about this mysterious man with the cat?"

"I don't think it's a man. That's your typical crystal ball smoke and mirrors. I'm guessing it's a pawn shop called The Cat's Whiskers. They have a sign with a black cat on it."

Suddenly Georgie got it. "I'm looking for the man who manages the pawnshop."

"No," Jerry said. "You're looking for the man who *owns* the pawnshop. Who would be Tim Taylor." He paused a moment, obviously relishing what he was about to reveal. "Madelyn Draper's lover."

That was a bombshell. They all stared at him in disbelief.

Georgie echoed everyone's thoughts. "Madelyn

Draper is having an affair with the owner of a pawn shop? Why would she risk that?"

"He doesn't manage it, just owns it. Along with half the real estate in the county. Richer than Douglas Draper, and a lot better-looking, which seems to be high on Madelyn's list of desirable qualities."

Georgie's head was spinning. "Jerry, how do you *know* all this?"

"Simple," Jerry said. "I sold Tim Taylor his motorhome. It had a few teething problems, and since Tim is one of our Platinum Care customers, I went to see to it personally. It was onsite at an exclusive RV resort—and guess who was there with him? She ducked out of sight when I arrived, but I knew who she was. I'd seen her enough times when I went out with Corinne."

Tammy finally spoke up. "As far as I can see, all of this is circumstantial. Madelyn might be playing away from home with this Tim Taylor, but how can we use that to prove Ricky's innocence?"

A somewhat feral glint entered Jerry's eyes. "How does Madelyn present herself to the world? As the society wife with a perfect life and perfect children. She rubs people's noses in it—and she doesn't hesitate to use people like Ossie McManus to stick the knife into others. What does she fear more than anything else? Social humiliation."

Scott, who had been following the conversation with his usual quiet attention, said: "You're planning to out her on Facebook?"

"The power of social media," Georgie said. "I like it. No police, no court cases."

"Not exactly," said Jerry. "We use the *threat* of social media. We'll use Madelyn's own not-so-secret weapon. Ossie McManus." He turned to Tammy. "Want to come with me and pay him a visit?"

CHAPTER 14

Exposed

At precisely two pm the next day, Tammy stood at the Draper household's front door for the second time in a week. This time, though, she had backup, flanked by Jerry on one side and Ossie McManus on the other.

She was looking forward to this.

Madelyn Draper opened the door to her three visitors. She looked suspiciously at Jerry and Tammy, and her eyes darkened when they rested on Ossie McManus. "This had better be good, Ossie. I canceled several appointments for you." She stepped back and motioned them inside. "What's so important that it had to be this afternoon?"

Ossie smiled at her. It was not a friendly smile. "Let's wait until we're all sitting down."

She flounced ahead of them, impatience in

every line of her body, and pointed to some easy chairs in the sitting room. "There." She perched on the edge of a leather recliner and looked at Ossie, ignoring Jerry and Tammy. "Well?"

Jerry spoke first. "Do you know who I am, Madelyn?"

"I've seen you at rallies for classic cars and trailers. You make vintage knockoffs." Her expression was disdainful, and her eyes went to Tammy. "It seems you're both good at that."

"I make million-dollar motorhomes, too," Jerry said. "Like the one we built for Tim Taylor."

She froze for a moment but recovered quickly. "Good for you."

"You might remember," Jerry went on, "that it had some teething problems when you went to Forest Lake. I had to adjust the lights and sound system?"

Madelyn pointedly ignored him and addressed Ossie. "Can we get to the point?"

"The point is," Ossie said, "you probably wouldn't want people to know that you're having an affair with Tim."

"I am not having an affair with Tim Taylor," she shot back. "Say so, and I'll sue."

"I don't have to say it in so many words. You know how it works, Madelyn. A whisper in the right ear; some old photos of you and Tim at social events…" Ossie shrugged. "You have a lot of enemies."

"Anyone in my position has enemies. People are envious." She narrowed her eyes at Ossie. "I'd be very careful if I were you, Ossie. You're not such an innocent yourself, are you?"

"You've held that threat over my head for years," Ossie said, spite in his eyes. "But you know what, Madelyn? For me, it would all blow over. But this, for you, would mean social disaster. Not to mention the end of your marriage."

"I doubt it." Madelyn was maintaining her arrogant attitude, but there was a light of panic in her eyes.

"Tim Taylor," Tammy said. "Your lover…and pawnshop owner. What story did you spin to get him to take your jewelry? Or did Tyler just do some sort of deal with the manager?" She tapped a finger thoughtfully on her bottom lip, looking at Ossie. "I guess the police will figure that one out."

Madelyn went white and stared at Tammy like a deer caught in the headlights.

"This is not going to play out well in the media, Madelyn," Ossie said with faux concern. "Framing your own son. Was it your idea, or Tyler's, to try planting drugs?" He shook his head. "I've been hoarding some little bits and pieces I've found out about Tyler. And that sister of his, Alexis. They're both up to their necks in it."

Abruptly, Madelyn stood up, staring down at him. "What do you want?"

"What I *want*," Ossie said, his voice full of dislike, "Is to see you behind bars. Along with your nasty nephew. But I've made an agreement with these two"—he jerked a thumb at Tammy and Jerry, sitting to his right, "to keep it under wraps for the sake of your kids. In return for you fixing it."

Relief warred with calculation in her eyes. "Fixing it how, exactly?"

"I don't know, and I don't care. Just makes sure the word gets out that it wasn't Ricky who stole your jewelry." Ossie pointed a finger at her. "I've got a lot on you now, Madelyn. Think of it as a time bomb. You step out of line, and it goes off."

"There's one more thing," Tammy said, watching her carefully.

Madelyn glared at her, her mouth tightening.

"We're telling Douglas."

"You. Will. Not." Madelyn bit the words out, striding over to stand in front of Tammy.

"Yes," Tammy said. "We will. He needs to know so that he can protect his children. Who knows what you'll dream up to hold against them in the future? You are a truly terrible mother."

"I'm not getting a divorce. No. He can't find out."

"There's always Tim Taylor in the wings," Tammy pointed out. "Rich. Good-looking. And bent, like you."

"Tim's just a friend. I like my life as it is, thank you," Madelyn said tightly.

"The problem is," Tammy shot back, "that your life is too good to be true. In fact, it's *not* true. It's all a fake." She smiled sweetly. "Like my dress."

Cornered, Madelyn stared at her, her fists clenching.

"Don't even think about it, Madelyn," Jerry said quietly, reaching across to take Tammy's hand.

"Go. All of you, leave."

"Happy to," Ossie said, standing up. "I'll be in touch to find out what your plans are."

Ten days later, Georgie's phone chirped, announcing a video call. The number coming up was Ricky Draper's.

When she answered, two homely faces wreathed in two identical broad smiles beamed at her.

"Hi, Ricky. Charlie." She grinned at them. "How's life?"

"You did it." Charlie's voice was jubilant. "They said they know it wasn't Ricky! Georgie, thank you! Thank you so much!"

"I had a lot of help," Georgie told her. She winked. "See, the good guys *do* win through."

"Just like you promised, Ricky's here for my birthday!"

Realization dawned. "You're thirteen today? Happy birthday, Charlie! That's fantastic!"

"I've started my Facebook page. Bethie nagged me into it. That photo of us all together is the first one I posted!"

Georgie beamed at her. "Terrific! I'll friend you."

"And Ricky's going to turn me into a character for one of his games!"

"Better and better," approved Georgie. "You can be a superhero."

"I'm going to be a magic dwarf." Charlie glanced at Ricky. "Which does have superpowers, doesn't it, Ricky? But the dwarf has a weakness too. Ricky says that everyone has to have a flaw."

"That way, she has to fight harder for what she wants," Georgie agreed. Her eyes met Ricky's, acknowledging the hidden message.

"Dad's so happy it wasn't Ricky," Charlie went on, switching back to the main topic. "He says he always believed in him. It was just...Mom." Her voice dipped on the last word. "But Mom's gone away for a while. She says she and Dad need a break from each other. Jonathan went with her."

Ricky said nothing but ruffled his sister's hair.

Georgie could tell he knew the truth.

Charlie would no doubt find out one day. Meanwhile, she was surrounded by people who loved her and believed in her: Ricky, her father, her sister.

Now that Charlie had had her say, Ricky spoke up. "Let me add my thanks to Charlie's, Georgie. I owe you."

"I was happy that we could help."

"I've talked to Ossie," he went on, with another glance at Charlie. "I don't think anything like this will happen again."

"Good." Like Ossie, Georgie would have been happy to see Madelyn dragged in to answer questions in a police interview room, but she'd settle for seeing Ricky Draper cleared and Charlie happy. "Tell me when the video game is out, guys. I can't wait to see Charlie the Magic Dwarf in action!"

She ended the call, smiling, just as Scott came in.

"Good news?" he asked.

"Ricky and Charlie. Madelyn's taken off somewhere, and their life has taken a turn for the better."

"Excellent," he said. "I've just been talking to Jerry, and it sounds like he and Tammy are back on track."

Georgie sighed, thinking of her brother. Could people really change? "For the moment," she said.

"They'll be OK," he said comfortably. "Jerry won't let her go. Tammy's pure gold." He slung an arm around her shoulder. "Like you. My favorite gypsy sleuth."

She laughed. "Another case closed."

"Until the next time that crystal ball calls to you."

"Until the next time," she agreed.

Life was always going to be interesting, waiting to see what came her way. Meanwhile, she had Scott, good friends, and the cutest toy poodle in the world.

Indeed, her life was almost too good to be true.

Next in This Series
AS GOOD AS IT GETS

Chapter 1

"Wow," Georgie said, staring down at the explosion of color in the field below. "I didn't know it was so big."

"It wasn't always," Scott said. "But that's what winning twenty-seven million will do."

Georgie's gaze tracked across the bright tents, the gaily painted RVs and trailers, the striped Big Top, the sideshows, the giant sign that sat over the wide entrance bordered by neat white picket fences: *Callaway's Flying Circus*. Underneath that, in slightly smaller letters, written in italic font, were the words "*& Carnival*".

"How many people work here?"

"Not sure. Fifty? Sixty? Plus the kids."

"Wow," she said again. "I always wanted to run away and join the circus. Doesn't every kid?"

Scott laughed. "Performing as what? A clown? Bearded lady?"

"I did gymnastics until I was ten," Georgie said, taking a swipe at him. "I wasn't exactly one of the stars, but who knows? With training, I could have been a trapeze artist. Maybe." Then her eye measured the size of the Big Top, and she thought about how she had never been any good with heights. "Or maybe not."

Behind them, the sound of a motor grew closer, and there was a crunch of gravel as a vehicle pulled off the road and stopped behind her gypsy trailer. She could tell it was Jerry's motorhome before she turned around.

Tammy was following close behind, towing her vintage trailer. She pulled off the road too, and they both got out to join Georgie and Scott.

Tammy came to stand beside Georgie. "Wow."

"That's what I said," agreed Georgie. "It looks amazing."

Jerry stood behind Tammy, with his hands on her shoulders. "Just think, we built half of those RVs and trailers. And Rollo Callaway is so thrilled with them he tells the whole world he bought them from Johnny B. Goode. You can't pay for that kind of advertising."

"I always wanted to join the circus," Tammy said, making Georgie laugh.

"See?" she said, elbowing Scott. "*Everyone* wants to do it at some time."

They stood for another few moments, drinking it in. Georgie could feel the same excitement she'd always felt as a kid when a circus or carnival came to town. Death-defying aerial acts, noise and music, the thrill of the amusement rides. Callaway's Flying Circus (& Carnival) didn't have any rides; it focused on performance arts and sideshows: trapeze artists, tumbling, trampoline, aerial silk, contortionists, stilt walkers, and fire eaters. And, of course, clowns and jugglers who did tricks and joined in the tumbling and gymnastics. Then there were the sideshows and booths: knife throwing, an illusionist, shooting gallery, knock em downs, and food stands.

Callaway's Circus also had a gypsy fortune-teller.

A gypsy fortune-teller who was, apparently, not much good at what she did. She was the reason Georgie had been asked to come along.

Her gaze moved to the lone gypsy trailer parked at the end of sideshow alley, between the sideshows and the fenced-off row of RVs and trailers that were the circus folks' home on the road.

Georgie gave a small sigh. How could you *train* someone to tell the future?

She had her doubts about whether it could be done at all, but the Callaways were paying the Johnny B. Goode RV Empire vast sums of money to get everything right—including giving some tips to their new fortune-teller. So here she was.

Under protest, but here.

"Well," she said, "I guess we'd better go down and meet them all."

"Guess so," agreed Scott, rubbing her upper arm reassuringly. "She might be just like you. You didn't know anything before Rosa gave you her crystal ball."

"Mmf," Georgie said, thinking instead about Rosa's mother, her great-great-grandmother. She had cheerfully made up fortunes just to earn money without being able to see any further than that night's dinner menu. What if this girl was just the same?

She *couldn't* be a party to promoting a fake fortune-teller.

"We'll see," she said. "Let's go find the Callaways."

Theodora Callaway was tall, loud, and dramatic. A swinging bell of chin-length hair, colored a defiant rich red, formed a contrast to the sweeping dark wings of her eyebrows and the bright blue of her eyes. She moved with the grace of a former dancer, but Georgie guessed that she had probably once been a gymnast like the rest of the family.

Jerry and Tammy had met the Callaways several times before, working with them on design and fit-out. Georgie could feel her brother's eyes on her, with barely-concealed amusement, when he introduced her to Theodora.

"Ah, you're the fortune-teller!" she boomed, extending a hand bedecked in rings and jangling silver bracelets. "Excellent. Ginger needs a guiding hand. I've always felt that she had a gift, but she won't listen." She clapped Georgie on the shoulder. "You'll sort her out."

Georgie smiled. "I look forward to meeting her."

A voice, tinged with annoyance and resentment, broke in. "I'm right here, Mom. You don't have to talk about me as though I'm some kid in the naughty corner."

Theodora gave an exaggerated start. "Ginger! I didn't see you there."

"Yeah, right." A slightly built woman with strawberry-blonde hair caught back in a braid moved in from the fringes of the swelling group of Callaways. They were flooding from everywhere, attracted by the arrival of a new gypsy trailer and the big black and gold Johnny B. Goode motorhome piloted by Jerry. Tammy's cheerful red and white vintage trailer was attracting its share of admiring glances, too, although nobody seemed very interested in Scott's humble truck camper.

Ginger narrowed her eyes at Georgie, not offering a hand. "I'm Ginger, and this is all Mom's bright idea."

Georgie kept her voice mild. "I'm not pushing anything at you, Ginger. Let's just talk and see where it leads." She smiled at her. "Fortune-telling isn't for everyone."

Theodora raised a finger and stabbed in the general direction of the circus's brand new gypsy trailer. "Too late. We've got the gypsy wagon waiting." She cast a quelling look at her daughter. "You can't do the aerial work anymore, so it might as well be fortune-telling."

Georgie felt her hackles rise, and her smile faded. It "might as well be fortune-telling"? She didn't mind it when people challenged her on what she did, but she *did* mind when they relegated the Sight to a low-grade parlor trick. Feeling Ginger's eyes on her, she held back from a retort.

What had happened to stop Ginger from doing aerial work? She'd have to find out.

A man with the same general body shape as Ginger edged around Theodora to introduce himself. He vibrated with energy, almost bouncing on his feet. "I'm Rollo Callaway," he said, grinning.

His eyes were hazel and kind, with deep laughter lines. "General manager and go-fer, husband of Theodora, father of Ginger, Darcy, Cassandra, and Oscar." He pointed at each one of his children as he said their names. "Since you're here for the week, you'll get to know them."

Georgie and Scott shook hands, nodded, and smiled as they worked their way around the group. The only one of the children to echo his mother's height was Darcy, who was dark and athletic, with an aerialist's knotted shoulder muscles. He shared Theodora's bright blue eyes, as did the youngest daughter Cassandra. Like her father, Cassandra radiated energy. "Our star performer," Rollo said proudly, patting his daughter on the head. "What she can't do with aerial silk, nobody can."

Georgie didn't miss the quick flash of hurt in Ginger's eyes at the words and her sideways glance at her brother Oscar, who was standing patiently waiting for the introductions to end. He seemed to be a miniature version of his father, but still and quiet. He put his hand briefly on Ginger's arm, an empathetic touch.

Interesting family dynamics.

"And these two are my two of our newest additions, Angelique and her brother Travis," Rollo went on. "Good all-round performers, both of them, but Angelique excels on the high wire while Travis does aerial silk and tumbling."

Blonde Angelique gave a brief nod, looking bored, and red-haired Travis stepped forward to shake hands with an engaging smile.

"Might as well do the tour," Rollo went on, flinging out an arm to encompass the entire circus. "Come on; I'll show you around. After all these years, we've finally made it." His face shone with pride. "This, folks, would have to be as good as it gets!"

The next hour passed in a whirl of being introduced to other performers and laborers and a whole bunch of assorted children as they toured the circus setup, from Theodora and Rollo's 1.3 million dollar RV to the Big Top. Then every booth from the hot dog stand to the cotton candy machine.

Finally, Rollo ran out of steam. "You'll be wanting to set up," he said. "Jerry, after you've had a break, come find me." He grinned. "You know where I live. I'll give you a list of the fixes we need —perhaps we can get started on those in the morning? Our first performance is tomorrow night, and then it's a busy week until we move on."

"Sure," Jerry said easily. "Unless there's anything urgent you want me to look at before dinner?"

Rollo nodded. "The water pump in Cassandra's bathroom, maybe, and the general drainage there. There's a leak. The rest can wait until tomorrow. You'll join us for a cookout tonight?"

"Thanks." After a glance around, Jerry accepted on behalf of all of them. "OK, I'll come and see you soon."

They all dispersed, but in the background, Georgie could see Ginger leaning against the hot dog stand with her arms folded, watching them.

She did not look happy.

Find it at your preferred bookstore or online: https://books2read.com/As-Good-As-It-Gets

I hope you have enjoyed the sixth book in the "Georgie" series and seeing the Crystal Ball Investigation Team at work again, helping Georgie solve a mystery and help the innocent. (I have to say that just reading about Tammy's 1920s clothes made me itch to go buy some for myself! One of my fave eras….)

Stay tuned for Georgie's next adventure in *As Good as it Gets*, a story set in the world of a traveling circus. Georgie and her little band of sleuths have to be very, very careful while they try to work out who they can trust… make sure you read the sample chapter in this book!

Here's an invitation for you: subscribe to my newsletter to get news of new releases, bonus books, specials and a sneak peek at scenes from my books in progress. As a welcome gift, you'll also receive a copy of *Fortune's Wheel*, the prequel to the Georgie series.

Here's your chance to find out more about the intriguing old woman that Georgie sees as a kind of taciturn genie. Whether she wanted to believe it or not, from birth Georgie was destined to follow in

Great-Grandma Rosa's footsteps—as well as inherit her crystal ball!

If you haven't already done so, visit my website below to join other readers and download your copy.

MargMcAlister.com/free-georgie-book/

ABOUT THE AUTHOR

Marg McAlister is the author of the popular Georgie B. Goode Cozy Mystery series (set in the USA) and Series 2 (Australian RV Adventure series), also featuring Georgie.

Marg lives by the sea on the mid-north coast of NSW, but she and her husband spend part of the year on The Gemfields in Central Queensland, living off the grid on their mining claim. While her husband digs for sapphires and zircons, operates the wash plant and drives around dirt tracks, Marg is usually writing—or socializing!

Marg is also the author of a series of books for aspiring writers, and the owner of Blue Gem Publishing, which publishes books in a range of genres.